PLAYED BY THE BILLIONAIRE (BILLIONAIRE ADVENTURERS)

AN ENEMIES TO LOVERS ISLAND ROMANCE

HARRIET POPE

Elina was stuck with Bernard on his private island and there was no way she could leave.

He was a total dick.

Sure he was good looking, had amazing eyes, and muscles that didn't stop. Hell, he was a God, but that didn't make him any more likeable.

He was a total player and his photo was always in all the gossip rags. He was, in fact, the last kind of man she would ever get involved with.

But that hadn't stopped him.

When she'd continued to refuse him, he'd used his friendship with his boss to get her this assignment. Made it impossible in fact for her to refuse if she wanted that promotion.

Dick!

So here she was on his bloody island and he was being just as impossible as he always was. Now she had to write a series of articles on him and he was making it take forever. On purpose.

She knew his game. With nowhere to go he was sure he'd wear her out in the end.

Well, he was wrong.

He was the kind of man who did nothing for her (regardless of the tingles but that was purely physical.) and there was no way she was ever going to climb into his bed.

Her sleep with him? Not bloody likely.

ONE

Was there going to be no bloody end to this fucking assignment?

Alina looked out angrily at the beach.

Yes, it was beautiful here. She had to admit that, and at some other time, with some other man, she would have enjoyed it.

But not with him. Definitely not with him.

He was the most spoilt, arrogant, conceited bloody bastard she'd ever met, and it was just her bloody luck to be stuck here with him, here on his private island, miles away from anywhere, with just a couple of native servants to keep them company.

Not that they were much company.

They must do their work in the middle of the night, she thought, *because other than being introduced to them when she'd first arrived she hadn't seen hide or hair of them since.*

The only person she saw - constantly - was him.

He was totally insufferable, and she couldn't count the amount of times she'd felt like telling him where he could shove it, but she was here to do this bloody job and part of it involved keeping the client happy, though she had no intention of doing it the way he had made clear he wanted.

For some crazy reason he'd set his cap at her.

God only knew why. She certainly had done everything to discourage him, though thinking about it, that had probably been where she went wrong Alina thought glumly.

Everyone knew a man liked a challenge and he was probably just as bad if not worse than all the others.

The more someone said "No" to him the more he was determined to turn that into "Yes Please".

So now what the hell was she supposed to do?

She was definitely running out of ideas.

She'd tried ignoring him, being cold and distant, and avoiding him, though the latter had no chance of working since she was here to work with him.

Alina sighed. All she wanted was to just go home.

She still didn't understand why Gerald had insisted she take this bloody assignment. She knew of at least ten other women who would have jumped at the chance.

Why hadn't he just given it to one of them?

She didn't want it, had never wanted it, and the longer she had to be here the more she felt that way.

But unfortunately, she was stuck here, Alina thought, sighing to herself again. *So, all she could really do was make the best of it.*

If she had to be here she might as well concentrate on the job and just get it done. The sooner she did that the sooner they could leave.

Or so she hoped.

Since he was the one who had ordered the pilot to come back for them in a week's time surely, he could also order him to come back earlier once they were finished.

But that meant they had to get this bloody thing written and it wasn't going to write itself. She still needed his input to finish it, so she really had no choice.

He might drive her crazy, but she had absolutely no choice.

She eyed the mini bar that had been set up on a cart in her room. What she wanted was a good stiff drink but that probably wasn't wise.

Not when she had to see him again. She needed all her wits about her.

She'd just have to order some tea, she thought with another sigh, and picking up her purse with resignation, she turned, determined now towards the door.

* * * *

He was sitting in the library having a drink when she walked in and smiled at her that famous smile she'd seen on all those magazine covers and in countless newspaper articles.

No point in thinking that's going to work with me buddy, she thought, looking at him and doing her best to look professional.

Putting her purse down on the table next to her notepad, she sat down, then looked at him.

"So, are you finally ready to work?" she asked him, trying not to sound sarcastic.

He'd been putting her off all day and it was three o'clock and they hadn't managed to get a bloody thing done.

"Why don't you have a drink first?" he said to her, still smiling at her,

"Might relax you a bit."

"I don't need to relax, thank you very much," she said, still looking at him.

"I'm here to do a job, not on vacation."

. . .

She could feel herself getting annoyed again but with determination she told herself to keep cool.

"No reason why you can't do both," he replied, and his eyes were laughing now.

"It'll be evening soon. I was thinking we'd have dinner out on the terrace. It should be a beautiful evening. Then maybe we can take a walk along the beach."

She looked at him, stunned. This man was unbelievable!

"What about working?" she asked him, and she could hear the anger creeping into her voice.

Don't go there. She told herself. *He's not worth it. Don't let him goad you.*

Taking a deep breath, she looked at him again.

She'd try to reason with him, though God knew he wasn't likely to respond to that either.

But what other options were left? She'd tried just about everything else.

"Look, Bernard," she said, making herself keep her voice nice and steady.

"You hired me to write this piece for you. I can't do it alone. You have to give me the information I need otherwise it won't get done."

"Is that what you want? Because if it is just phone your pilot and tell him to come back and pick me up. I'm just wasting my time here."

He looked at her seriously for a minute, then he slowly smiled again.

"Okay. You're right. You need to do this. I'll answer your questions, so you can start working on it in the morning while I'm in the gym, but in return I want you to have dinner with me, take a walk on the beach with me afterwards, and act as if you're enjoying it."

He looked at her seriously.

"I'm not such a bad guy you know. I can be fun once you get to know me. How about giving me a chance? One evening." he said, still smiling.

"Well, to start with anyway. What do you say?"

This man is bloody impossible, she thought. *The last thing I want to do is spend an evening with him. And look like I'm enjoying it? He's got to be kidding.*

But she really didn't have a choice here.

At least he'd promised to cooperate if she did and it would be the first time in the last two days that she might actually get something done.

Looking at him with resignation, she answered him, but she didn't smile. He'd said she was to pretend she was enjoying the dinner. Right now, she definitely wasn't enjoying this, and looking like she did wasn't part of the deal.

"Fine. You've got a deal." She said, looking down at her

so far empty notepad, and grabbing her pencil she looked back at him again.

"So, you ready to answer some questions?"

"Shoot," he said, sitting back in his chair, his eyes on her still.

Alina looked down at the list and read the first question she'd prepared.

"Your friends all call you Bear. Is there a specific reason? Is it a childhood nickname or something?

He was grinning now.

"Nope, not a childhood nickname. More a current one."

"So, why?" she persisted.

"Probably because I'm hung like a Bear."

She looked at him, stunned. Had he really said that?'

"You're joking, right? I can't print that. That's disgusting!"

He was grinning at her wickedly now.

"None of the ladies seem to think so. Want to check it out for yourself?"

Alina looked down at the table and took another deep breath. At this rate they would get exactly nowhere.

She pulled herself together and looked at him.

"Look, if you want me to take this deal seriously then you've got to do your part. Either give me something I can print or let's just forget this whole bloody thing."

. . .

He was still looking at her and grinning, and she felt like slapping him across the face.

God, he was insufferable! How the hell was she going to stand him for another week?

He obviously could see in her eyes that she was very close to losing it because suddenly he got serious.

"Look Ally. I'm sorry. It's just so much fun to rile you up. You're so gorgeous when you're angry.

But you're right. I'll get serious now. The sooner we do this the sooner we can get to the fun part of the evening."

Still looking at her seriously he asked quietly.

"What do you want to know?"

Not really believing he was going to answer them any more seriously than he had the first one, she asked him the rest of her questions and he surprised her.

He gave her all the information she needed and as she scribbled furiously on her notepad she marveled at how changeable this man was.

How could someone change so completely so suddenly?

One minute he was an idiot playboy without a serious bone in his body and the next he was sitting there across from her looking for all the world like the extremely successful businessman she knew he was.

It was mind blowing really, but she was just thankful he'd finally gotten serious.

As for the rest of the evening, well she'd deal with it somehow. It was only going to be a few hours.

She'd handled worse. She could deal.

After half an hour she had more than enough to start, and reluctantly she looked up at him.

"Thanks," she said quietly. "This will definitely give me enough to get started tomorrow."

"Good," he said, getting up and smiling at her.

"Now go get ready for our evening. It's formal and I know you didn't bring formal clothes, so I made sure some were sent to your room. I'm pretty sure you'll find they're the right size. I'm pretty good at making estimations." He added, and his eyes gleamed wickedly at her.

"Dinner will be at eight." He said, speaking softly. "I'll come and get you. Wouldn't want you to get lost."

Then giving her one last smile, he turned and walked out of the room.

Alina sat back with a deep sigh and took another sip of her now cold tea.

She definitely wasn't looking forward to this evening, but a deal was a deal, and at least he'd cooperated and given her what she needed.

Finally, but hey, beggars can't be choosers.

TWO

The first thing Alina saw when she let herself into her room was the clothes rack.

He'd sent her three dresses to choose from, and as she looked at them she noticed that even though they were different colors and different styles, they were really all the same.

Made out of a clingy silk that was so thin it was almost not there, they were long, yes, but they were also all strapless with very little back.

Shit! she thought, *I can't wear any of these. Besides, I don't have the right underwear.*

Then she noticed the plastic bag lying on the shelf above the dresses.

It contained a strapless bra and a thong.

Made of fine lace the set was beautiful, but it certainly wasn't going to hide much she thought with a sigh.

There were a pair of silver heeled sandals and a small

matching evening purse lying next to the bag, and that was it.

She was tempted to ignore the clothes and just wear her regular daytime business attire.

She was here on business for Christ's sake! Not to play dress-up doll for him, but as she fingered the silk on the light blue dress, she couldn't help being tempted.

No doubt about it, it was a beautiful dress. She wasn't likely to get to wear something like this again. What could it hurt? It was only for a few hours.

* * * *

As she lay in her bath, enjoying a well-deserved soak, Alina couldn't help thinking how different all this was from what she was used to.

She'd been lucky. She'd grown up in a happy home with an older brother and sister and two wonderful parents.

Family life had always been important to them and she'd loved seeing how lovingly her parents treated one another, even after all these years, and she'd been determined that one day she wanted what they had.

Her father had owned a hardware store and her mother had stayed at home, so there was never a lot of money.

They were comfortable, but there hadn't been many luxuries when she was growing up.

Not that she'd really felt like she was missing out Alina thought. There wasn't a lot, but there had always been enough, and since they were all healthy, happy, and together, they had always felt blessed.

Unfortunately, she hadn't experienced anything like that so far with any of the men she'd dated.

Not even close.

She was very attractive, slim, with long blond hair and blue eyes and she always had her choice of men to go out with.

Even though they had all been attractive, intelligent, and she'd enjoyed their brief relationships, she'd never been even remotely tempted to take those relationships any further.

Much as she'd had a good time, none of them had really done it for her.

She'd never met anyone who had made her feel even remotely like her Mom felt about her Dad, and that was what she wanted. She just couldn't settle for anything less and if that meant she would end up alone, well, so be it.

There were worse options, she thought, *like ending up being a plaything for a man like Bernard.*

Yes, he was very smart and very successful.

He was also incredibly handsome, she couldn't deny that, but his whole personality, his whole way of living totally put her off, and when it came down to it, she really couldn't see why all those women always flocked to him.

Probably his money, Alina thought with a sigh, *the man was definitely loaded, but did he really enjoy being with women who didn't really care for him? Who just wanted him for his money?*

Who knew? she thought, sighing again, *a man like that ....* *She had no idea what went through his head.*

She knew he got serious sometimes. He wouldn't be as successful as he was if he didn't.

He'd finally shown her some of that side, but he was also a total Lech. He seemed to have a massive sexual appetite going on the string of women she'd seen pictured with him, and he was used to getting what he wanted, but when it came to her, he could totally forget it.

A man like him did absolutely nothing for her.

All she wanted was to get this bloody assignment done and over with, so she could go home.

Giving one last sigh, Alina got out of the tub and started to get ready for their evening.

He knocked on her door exactly at eight o'clock, and when she opened her door to him she caught her breath in surprise.

Fuck! She'd known he was good looking, but in a tux .... *He was stunning. If you could say a man was stunning,* she thought to herself. *He'd definitely stunned her.*

As she looked up at him he softly smiled.

"You chose the blue one. Good choice. That was my

favorite. I knew it would look amazing on you. It shows of your beautiful blue eyes."

He just stood there looking at her, and starting to feel uncomfortable, Alina backed away.

Shit! she thought, *she hadn't thought about the fact that he'd chosen these clothes personally. That he'd seen the underwear she was wearing, maybe even held the smooth lace in his fingers, and was probably picturing her in it now when he looked at her.*

She felt cold shivers going up and down her spine.

"I'll just grab my purse." She mumbled. He was starting to really affect her, and she definitely didn't like this.

This wasn't what she'd signed up for.

As she walked out of her room and closed the door, he put his arm around her, and led her towards the stairs. She was very aware of the feel of his hand on her naked back, and she was definitely starting to feel very uncomfortable, but she told herself to be sensible.

It's just one bloody dinner. Alina told herself sternly. *It's not like you've never been out with an attractive man before. He's no different from any of the others.*

That's what she kept telling herself, but she knew she was wrong.

He might not be her type, in fact definitely wasn't her type, but there was something different about him. Much as she didn't want to, she was starting to feel something when she was with him.

She had no idea what it was. Most of the time he drove her completely up the wall, so surely, she couldn't be attracted to him in any way.

No, it was just probably the weirdness of this whole situation, she told herself.

She might have been out to dinner with clients many times before, but these had been definite business dinners, held in busy restaurants, and she'd been properly dressed for the occasion.

This was something completely different.

She was here with him, alone, and she was wearing a dress that was hardly there. One that she was uncomfortably aware showed him a lot more of her body than she really wanted him to see.

When he reached the main floor, instead of turning towards the library where she usually spent her days with him, he turned in the other direction. She hadn't seen this part of the house and she looked around with interest.

He certainly lives in the height of luxury, she thought.

Even though they were on an island, miles away from anywhere, you wouldn't know it by his home. There was everything here he could possibly want .... and a hell of a lot more.

The room he led her into was huge.

Furnished with comfortable sofas and deep chairs set up in small conversation groupings, the well-polished wood floor gleamed between the many Persian rugs that were scattered over it.

On one side there was a long bar with half a dozen stools and she could see the well-stocked glass shelves above it, reflecting the multitude of bottles. Next to it stood a large pool table and a holder with pool cues was attached to the wall above.

It was all very beautifully furnished, beautifully accessorized, but what really took her breath away was the fireplace.

Located on the far wall, it was massive, built of stone and reaching to the ceiling, it was huge.

Though when they would ever have need of a fireplace here was beyond her, Alina thought. *It was always so hot.*

In front of it was a large white fur rug, and this made her smile.

Typical. She thought. *Isn't that what you found in every seduction scene she'd ever read? When it came down to it, this man was so bloody typical.*

The room was definitely beautiful, but Bernard didn't linger. He guided her through the French doors on the other side of the room and she found herself on the terrace.

But what a terrace!

. . .

Built out of the same stone they had used on the fireplace, it was massive and seemed to reach all around to the side of the house.

It was filled with a multitude of flowering plants in beautiful oriental pots, and together with the scent from the flower garden below them, they perfumed the air.

The house was built on the side of a hill, and as she stood taking it all in, Alina looked at the view.

It was really amazing.

It was dark now, but the water shimmered in the moonlight, and she could see the outline of the palm trees that lined the beach, their fronds swaying in the light breeze.

She was starting to feel overwhelmed. She'd known he was rich.

Very rich, but this? It was bloody amazing.

She could understand how women would be bowled over by the whole setting once he got them here, but the bottom line was he was never serious about any of them as far as she could see and that was pretty obvious.

He was just out to get laid, so why would they even bother going there?

He was a total waste of time as far as she was concerned and no woman in her right mind would think anything else.

But she had to admit this whole setup was pretty impressive, and if she was really honest, she could see the appeal of letting yourself get lost in all this, even if it was temporary.

Not for you. She reminded herself sternly. *You're here to do a job and that's it. This man is definitely not for you.*

But the fact that she was even remotely considering it in any way was definitely disturbing.

THREE

The table was set up just in front of the stone terrace wall, and as he held the chair for her and she sat down, she could see the flower garden below them.

Even though it was dark, there were lights subtly illuminating it, and a path ran through it winding its way down to the beach. It reminded her that she'd also agreed to walk on the beach with him.

Alina turned back to the table with resignation.

She'd promised to look as if she was enjoying this. It wasn't going to be easy but maybe if she concentrated on the surroundings and tried to forget the man she could manage it.

Not that doing that was going to be all that easy either. In fact, she had a feeling it was going to be damn hard, but she'd just have to do it.

It was only one evening, she reminded herself. *She'd spent*

evenings with people she didn't care for before and had to be
charming. She could do it with him. How hard could it be?

Determined now, she turned to him with a smile.

"It's beautiful out here. It certainly is a gorgeous night."

He just looked at her and smiled. She had a feeling he knew exactly what she was doing but he was going along with her, making small talk just as she was. Maybe this wouldn't be too bad.

The dinner was amazing.

For the first time in the two days she'd been there she actually saw someone else. Edwardo was obviously an islander, and as Bernard laughed and joked with him after introducing him, Alina watched him silently.

He definitely treated his servants well. He always introduced them, never spoke down to them, and that really impressed her.

She'd known a few other people who were well off, attended a few dinner parties at their homes, and had always hated the way they spoke to their servants.

They treated them like possessions. Just one more thing they'd bought and paid for, but Bernard wasn't like that at all.

Any time she'd seen him talking to any of the natives he'd always been friendly and polite and treated them like the real people they were.

Yes, he paid their salary and she was sure he didn't think twice about demanding what he was paying for, but he did it in a nice way and this was definitely a point in his favor.

Though when she'd started to keep a score card was beyond her.

What did any of this matter to her anyway?

It wasn't as if he was going to be part of her life after this week. Once this assignment was over she'd probably never see him again and that was a good thing. She really didn't need this aggravation.

She thoroughly enjoyed the wine, the seafood, and the fresh vegetables that were grown by his gardener, and as she ate her Creme Brûlée and sipped her coffee she realized she was actually enjoying this, not just pretending.

She wasn't that sure about the next part of the evening.

Walking with him on the beach?

She wasn't at all sure that was such a good idea, but at least the dinner had gone very well.

As she finished eating her dessert she saw he was sitting back in his chair and just looking at her with those dark eyes of his.

There were too many moments when he was doing that now. Not saying anything, just looking at her, and it was really starting to make her uncomfortable. She'd managed to break the silence so far by making small talk, but there was only so much she could say.

"I'm glad you enjoyed the meal." He said quietly when she told him how good the food was. "Ready for our walk? "Then he got up and extended his hand to her.

She looked at him, really uncomfortable now.

He wanted to hold hands? But he didn't give her any time to think about it. When she didn't move he reached down and grabbed her hand, pulling her out of her chair, so she really had no choice but to go along with him.

He led her down the stone steps and into the garden. It was even more beautiful up close, and she breathed deeply, inhaling the heady scent that filled the air.

He was bloody lucky to have this place, she thought. *What an amazing getaway. I know he works hard but being able to come here and get away must make it a hell of a lot easier.*

Soon they were on the beach and as she stumbled along he laughed.

"Heels aren't meant for beach walking. Take them off."

He gave her that famous stare of his as he spoke, and even though he was only talking about shoes, his voice and the way he'd said it gave her tingles, and she could feel them running up and down her spine.

· · ·

Get a grip! She told herself sternly. *Do not let this man get to you. Remember, he's nothing but trouble. Even thinking about letting down your guard for even a minute would be bloody dangerous. Get a grip!*

He was still holding her hand and he'd stopped now, waiting for her to remove her shoes. As she bent down he put his arm around her, his fingers on her back, and the feel of them on her skin wasn't helping.

Fuck!, she thought. *This isn't going well.*

Walking away from him with determination she headed for a large sea shell she could see laying on the sand.

"This is gorgeous." She said, pretending to study it. She heard him laugh, and when she looked up he'd walked over to her again.

"Not as gorgeous as you are." He said, smiling down at her, and stroking her face. "Especially when you're playing hard to get."

He leaned down, obviously meaning to kiss her, but she quickly moved away, then she looked at him, determined now.

"I'm not playing Bernard." She said. "I'm here on business. Please remember that." He laughed again.

"Whoever said you can't mix business with a little pleasure was definitely wrong."

He walked up to her then slowly, and taking her hand, he kissed it, his eyes on her still."

"But I'm not going to push you Ally. When you finally

come to my bed I want you there willingly. I want you to want me, just as much as I want you."

Fuck! This man doesn't beat around the bush, Alina thought, then still determined, she looked back at him.

"It's not going to happen Bernard." She said. He was still looking at her with that smile of his.

"Oh yes, it will Love," he said.

"One of these days, very soon, it will. And I can wait. Waiting for what you want makes it that much more enjoyable once you finally get it."

Then kissing her hand again, he turned and continued walking down the beach, still holding her hand firmly in his.

So not going to happen, Alina said to herself firmly. *So not going to happen.*

But deep inside she was starting to feel herself weaken.

He wasn't her kind of man at all. He was bloody dangerous in fact. But there was something about him that was starting to get to her and it was starting to really scare her.

The sooner she could get this bloody article written the better.

She really needed to get out of here before she did something she would always regret.

FOUR

As Alina sat in the library the next morning working on her article, she couldn't help thinking about the previous night.

After saying what he had on the beach he'd been a perfect gentleman.

He'd talked and laughed with her while they walked, and she'd relaxed a little.

It was a beautiful night and it was a gorgeous setting. She couldn't really help but enjoy it, and when he was charming Bernard was very good company.

When he'd walked her to her room, she'd started to feel nervous again.

Was he going to try to kiss her again?

After what he'd said, what she now knew his end goal was, she was pretty sure that would be his next move, but again he surprised her.

. . .

When she turned to him after opening her door he was just standing there smiling at her, and as she told him goodnight and then held her breath, wondering what he was going to do next, he just kept looking at her, but his eyes had a suspicious twinkle.

After a minute he just took her hand and softly kissed it, then bidding her goodnight he turned and walked back down the hall.

She had a feeling he'd known all too well what she'd been expecting, and the way he kissed her hand now was more and more like a caress. Each time he lingered longer and each time it affected her more.

And he bloody well knows it, she thought. *She hadn't imagined that twinkle in his eyes. He was doing this on purpose. Keeping her guessing. Wondering when he would make his next move.*

It was all very unnerving.

Time to get to work, she told herself sternly. *If you want to get out of here then you'd better concentrate your energy on writing, not thinking about him.*

He constantly had his photo in all the newspapers and magazines, was very well known, and one of the large New York papers had wanted to run a three-part series on him.

He'd agreed but he'd insisted that he would choose who was going to write it, and since their company did his PR, it only made sense that he'd asked them to handle it. The information he'd given her would be enough for the first part of the series, but she would still have to get more from him for the rest.

Hopefully he'll cooperate like he did yesterday, she thought. *But there weren't going to be any more beach walks.*

He was very persuasive, very compelling, and more and more she found herself fascinated by him, and that wasn't good.

She had no desire to sleep with him but she was only human.

Any woman put into this kind of position was going to be vulnerable, and she had to protect herself from him as much as she could. When it came to beach walks she would have to draw the line.

If she was to have a prayer of resisting him she knew she couldn't put herself in that kind of position again.

Sighing, Alina brought her mind back to her writing. He'd said he'd be busy until ten. She wanted to get this first part written. At least the first draft.

* * * *

As he walked into the library and smiled at her, Alina looked back at him anxiously.

Would he continue to cooperate?

She certainly hoped so.

She'd finished the first part and she was happy with the way it had turned out. He had the last say so she'd give it to him to read when it was totally finished, but hopefully he wouldn't have a lot of changes.

. . .

Now she needed to get information for the second part.

The first installment was really a general introduction. Not that most people would need it. Most people knew who he was and what he did, but that was the way they always wrote these things because there were always some who would need the background.

The second section she was thinking she'd write on his family, then she could finish with a section on his business.

As he sat down in his chair and looked at her, she made herself smile at him.

"Ready to work again? The information you gave me yesterday was great. I've managed to write the first draft of the first installment. Now I'd like to get some information for the next one."

He looked at her and slowly he smiled again.

"Fine. I can do that. Same deal as yesterday." Then as she was going to protest, he looked at her knowingly.

"I had a feeling you wouldn't want to take another walk on the beach with me, so we can leave that part out." As she breathed a sigh of relief he continued, still smiling, but his eyes twinkled mischievously now.

"There are a lot of talented musicians on this island and some of them are very good. I've hired a group to play for us this evening while we have dinner." Then while she was thinking she could do that, he added,

"Instead of walking on the beach, after dinner we'll take advantage of the music and dance."

. . .

He sat back and looked at her, waiting for her reaction, his eyes still twinkling.

Bloody hell! She thought angrily, *he knows very well that I'm not going to like that anymore than walking with him on the beach.*

But she wasn't going to give him the satisfaction of seeing her flustered. This man was way too sure of himself.

"Fine." She said, doing her best to look as if she didn't really care. "So, ready to work?"

He just looked at her knowingly then, but he didn't pursue it any further.

As she asked him her new list of questions and he answered her, serious now, she made herself concentrate.

She could spend a few minutes dancing with him. It was no big deal. she told herself, but the truth was she had serious doubts.

He answered the first few questions without any problem and she was just congratulating herself on how well it was going when he suddenly got quiet on her.

She'd asked him about his family, and when she looked up at him his face had gone completely blank.

"Sorry. I don't talk about my family." He said, shortly. "It's not important. What's important is who I am now, not where I came from." Then as she looked at him questioningly, he added, sharply now. "Move on to the next topic."

. . .

Alina looked at him in surprise.

He'd changed completely yet again. Gone was the charming, friendly banter. He was all business now and his face was deadly serious.

She would have loved to ask him more, but somehow, she knew he wouldn't take it well.

With resignation she quickly decided she would have to change her plan. Obviously, the family thing was out.

Maybe she could write about his education instead. She moved on to those questions and he seemed genuinely relieved. As he answered her she could see him relax once more.

There's something strange there about his family, she thought. *I wonder why he won't talk about them?*

She'd already done some background research on him and it was true.

In everything she'd read there had never been any mention of them.

It was a puzzle, but she had a feeling, going on how short he'd been with her when she'd brought it up, that it wasn't one she'd be able to solve.

They worked for an hour and at the end Alina was starting to feel a lot more confident about this assignment.

After those awkward few minutes when she'd asked him about his family, he'd been quite happy to answer all the rest of her questions, and yet again she had more than enough information to get on with. Maybe this would all work out after all.

As she stood up and gathered up her notes, he walked up to her.

"Wear that blue dress again Alina." He said quietly, looking at her seriously. "It suits you, and I like seeing you in it. You'll find some clean under things on your bed."

He turned to go, then turned back to her, and he was smiling softly at her now.

"It needs something though to make it perfect. You'll find a jewelry case on your bed as well."

"Don't freak out on me." He added, and he was grinning now. "I'm not trying to bribe you into my bed with jewelry. It's only on loan. It belonged to my grandmother, but it will be perfect with that dress."

Turning serious again, he stroked her cheek.

"I think it will look perfect on you. You don't have to wear it if you don't want to, of course, but it would give me great pleasure to see it on you." Then still looking at her seriously, he turned and walked out.

As she dressed that night, Alina thought about their after-noon together. This man was definitely full of surprises.

That whole thing with his family was very strange. He was obviously very touchy about them. Which made the whole jewelry thing even stranger, she thought.

. . .

When she'd looked into the jewelry case she's seen it contained a beautiful sapphire and diamond necklace.

Not clunky or ostentatious as a lot of old jewelry seemed to be, this necklace was very delicate and very beautifully crafted.

The earrings were just very simple studs. Each one had a small sapphire surrounded by tiny diamonds.

She'd wondered at the wisdom of going along with his wishes, but in the end, she'd decided she would.

After all, he'd said it would make him happy. What could it hurt?

He came to collect her again, and seeing she was wearing the necklace and earrings, he softly smiled.

"You look wonderful." He said, softly. "I knew they would suit you." Then he put his arm around her and led her downstairs.

As she walked with him through the large living room she could hear the musicians already playing on the patio.

There were four of them, and as they walked out Bernard greeted them all by name and they smiled at him as they continued playing. Yet again she was impressed at the easy way he had with the people who worked for him.

The dinner was delicious just as before, and again he seemed quite content to make small talk as they ate, but as they were sipping their coffee after having finished their dessert, he smiled at her and she could see that mischievous twinkle was back in his eyes again.

"Ready for the dancing part?" he asked her, his eyes still twinkling.

"Sure," she replied, slowly getting up from her chair. How bad could this be?

He walked up and put his arms around her, then walking with her further down the patio, he led her in a slow waltz.

The only light was from the softly flickering candles on their table and the moon shining high above them.

As she listened to the music quietly playing, he tightened his arms around her, drawing her closer to him. One hand was on her back while the fingers of the other one tenderly caressed her, slowly making their way lower and lower down her body.

He guided her around the floor, then after a few minutes, he kissed the top of her head.

"You're so beautiful Ally." He murmured. "And God, I want you so much. If I can't have you in my bed yet, at least I can hold you in my arms."

Shit, she thought to herself, *this is so not a good thing to be doing.*

But she couldn't make herself draw away.

There was something about this man. Even though she hadn't wanted it, had done her best to fight it, there was something building between them, and it was getting stronger and stronger with each passing day.

. . .

That night when he walked her to her room he seemed especially quiet, and when she turned to him to say good-night, the look in his eyes was so intense it scared her.

"I have to go in now," she whispered, no longer sure what it was she was feeling.

"Not just yet." He said, still looking at her. Then he walked up until he was only inches away, and looked deeply into her eyes, searching now.

She knew what he wanted to know.

She knew this wasn't wise, knew she would probably regret it later, but she couldn't help herself any longer.

Regardless of how much she'd fought it, it had obviously been inevitable, and now it was too late. She wanted this. She'd fallen under his spell.

Seeing what he'd hoped to see, he bent his head and kissed her.

Softly at first, then groaning, he tightened his arms around her and kissed her again, much more passionately, and when she instinctively opened her lips for him, he swept inside, possessing her with an unflinching determination that made her want him even more.

She couldn't help herself.

Kissing him was so amazing, and she found herself kissing him back just as passionately. The longer she kissed him the more she could feel herself weakening.

· · ·

If he decides to follow me into my room, will I be able to turn him away? Probably not, she thought.

He was awakening a longing in her she hadn't known was there. Just a couple of days ago she'd hated the very sight of him.

Now she wanted him.

Seems he'd been right.

At this rate she would not only end up in bed with him, but she'd be more than willing. She wanted him now just as much as she could see he wanted her, and that really scared her.

She'd never been taken so unawares by anyone before. What was it about this man?

With determination, she made herself draw away. What was she doing here?

Did she really want to go down this path?

She needed to think about this before it went any further.

He was breathing heavily now, just as she was, and she could see how hard it was for him to let her go, but finally he did, his eyes still on her face.

"Goodnight Ally." He said softly, stroking her face again. "Sweet dreams," then with one last regretful look at her, he turned and walked away.

FIVE

Alina found it hard to sleep that night.

She couldn't help herself. All she could think about was that kiss, and she was still thinking about it as she sat down at the library table the next morning, her notes in a folder beside her and her laptop set up in front of her, all set up and ready for her to start writing the second installment in the series.

She had more than enough information, she knew exactly how she was going to write it, now all she needed to do was write, and she was sure she'd have this done again before he appeared.

She knew he spent an hour each morning in his private gym, then worked in his home office for a couple of hours so he could finish whatever business needed to be done for the day.

She had expected that, given what a busy man he was and how many pies he seemed to have his fingers in. In fact, she'd been amazed that he didn't work more, but he obviously had that part of his life very much in control just as he did the rest of it.

She'd found a coffee pot filled with fresh coffee already waiting for her, and as she sipped thankfully, her mind wandered yet again to that kiss.

How the hell had she fallen for this man?

Most of the time she didn't even like him. He was such a bloody know-it-all and so sure of himself.

But she was also starting to slowly see another side of him as well. A side that was caring, considerate, respectful, and much as she'd never believed it could ever happen, her opinion of this man was slowly changing.

Oh, he was still a playboy. That was something that she couldn't ignore.

He went through women like tissues and discarded them just as quickly once he'd gotten what he wanted. There was certainly no denying that.

The evidence stared up at her every time she opened a newspaper or looked at a magazine. But she was starting to see he wasn't what he seemed.

What you see isn't always what you get, she thought. *Sometimes there is much more,* and she had to admit to herself she was intrigued. She wanted to find out just how much more there really was.

. . .

That kiss had definitely blown her away.

She was obviously attracted to him. There was no way she could deny that any longer.

She'd come very close to inviting him into her bed and the thought of how close was definitely very scary.

How could her feelings for him change so quickly?

How could it be that a man she'd hated a few short days ago she now wanted just as passionately?

Alina had no idea.

She was twenty-eight, she might not be beautiful, but she knew that she was very attractive, and she'd gone out a lot more than most women her age.

She'd met a lot of guys and slept with her share of them.

She liked sex, and she'd enjoyed these relationships, even though none had lasted, but she'd never felt even remotely as taken by a man as she did with him.

At thirty-five he'd lived one hell of a life already and accomplished an amazing amount.

He was successful, rich, charming when he wanted to be, and undeniably incredibly good looking. He had his good points, she had to admit.

He still irritated her, and she couldn't imagine spending any length of time with him without killing him. Spending more than this week with him would probably drive her completely crazy, but she was here now.

She was here, and he'd made it very obvious that he wanted her.

. . .

She certainly wasn't kidding herself. She knew that once this week was over he'd probably forget all about her, never give her another thought, but right now she was here, so why not enjoy it?

She was deeply attracted to him and she wanted to know what it would be like to sleep with him, to have him make love to her. Just the thought of it sent cold shivers down her back. So why not?

It wasn't like she was in any danger of falling in love with him anymore than he was likely to fall in love with her.

They were just too different and lived completely different lives and in completely different worlds. In fact, it was amazing that they'd even managed to meet at all, but they had.

They'd not only met but Gerald had insisted that she go with him to his island on this assignment.

It had obviously been meant to be for some reason, so why fight it?

Certainly, once he stopped constantly thinking of ways to pursue her he would be more relaxed, he would have gotten what he wanted and would be ready to move on, so hopefully he'd be eager to help her finish this series, so they could leave.

She'd be able to go back to her life, Gerald would be happy, and hopefully she'd get that promotion she had her eye on.

Meanwhile she might as well enjoy herself.

. . .

He'd get what he wanted, she'd have a bit of a fling, and they'd both be happy. It was really the best solution. There was no point in fighting fate.

Having decided what she wanted to do, Alina turned her mind with determination to her work.

Once she started writing, Alina found herself getting more and more engrossed by it, so she looked up in surprise when she heard him walk in.

Was it ten o'clock already?

He sat down in his usual chair and smiled,

"How's it going today? Getting everything done?"

"It's going great," she replied smiling back. "I'm not quite finished, but almost.

I think this part will work out just as well as the first." The she looked at him in surprise.

"Are you ready to work already?" The clock on the library wall showed it was only nine thirty.

"No. Sorry." He said, still smiling. "There's been a change of plans."

She looked at him questioningly.

"I've got a Skype conference in a few minutes and it will probably be a long one. Then this afternoon I've got to go check on some things here on the island, so we won't be able to work today, but since you're really ahead of schedule, I think we can afford to take a break."

"Edwardo will bring you lunch so you can keep working. Once you finish what you want to do today, go change into some shorts and a light top. I want to take you with me.

You might as well see some of the island while you're here and it's too hot to be wearing much out there." Then he grinned wickedly.

"Oh, and wear a bikini under your clothes. Unless you'd prefer to just swim naked. I'm definitely up for that. "

"There's a nice little lake where we're going, and a swim will be refreshing today. "He explained, still grinning.

Quickly Alina made up her mind.

Hadn't she just decided there was no point in fighting fate? Besides, she wouldn't mind a break.

"Ok. Fair enough." She said, looking at him with a smile. "And seeing some of the island will be interesting. A break would be nice."

He looked slightly surprised.

Probably thought I was going to fight him yet again. Nice to see I can surprise him for a change. She thought, smiling to herself.

He was still looking at her, and grinning again now, he got up and turned to leave.

"Good. See you in a while." And with a parting smile, he walked out of the door.

He was right. She was ahead of schedule.

He'd planned for them to be here for a week, he'd told her he also had things to take care of here on the island while he was here so there really was no point in rushing.

Especially if she was going to sleep with him.

They would only have a few more days together anyway, but she might as well enjoy them. It would be a nice break.

SIX

He met her at the bottom of the stairs, and looking at her, he smiled.

"Yes, you'll be okay in that." He said as he eyed her shorts and top.

"Are you wearing your bikini?"

"Yes." She replied, and he smiled at her again, this time grinning wickedly.

"Good. Can't wait to see it." He said, quietly.

He knew exactly what it did to her each time he said things like that, and laughing at her knowingly, he took her by the arm, leading her outside.

There was an old battered green jeep standing on the drive, and as he opened the door for her, she saw it had definitely been through the wars.

The leather seats were well-worn, and the sides of the car were scratched and scraped, the paint having been removed completely in some places, leaving just the metal frame gleaming at her.

Not what I expected, she thought, surprised, but then she didn't really know what she'd expected.

They were, after all, going to be driving around the island and she'd never been on a small island like this one before, so she really had no clue what to expect.

So far, she'd only seen the small air strip where the plane had landed, and the drive to the house had been along the coast and only a few minutes long.

From what he'd said while they were flying here in his private Jet, she knew the island was only a few miles wide and not much longer.

He'd told her there was one village with one small school, one hospital, and one grocery store. Other than that, there were a few houses scattered here and there, but most of the island inhabitants lived in the village.

There was a small sugar cane plantation, a small factory that made rum, and that was it. There really was no other industry here, and since he owned the whole island, and that included both the sugar cane plantation and the rum factory, most of the people living here worked for him in some capacity or other.

The road to the village wound through the jungle, but here and there they would come out by the ocean, and she could

see there were several beautiful beaches, completely unin-
habited, the ocean waves lapping on the golden sand
sparkling in the sunlight, the tall palm trees surrounding
them swaying gently in the light breeze.

It really is beautiful here, she thought again as she
marveled once more at how rich this man must be to be able
to afford all of this.

After half an hour of navigating carefully on the rut-filled
road, Bernard finally drove them into the village, and as she
looked around curiously, she saw that, just as he'd said, it
wasn't very big at all, but it certainly looked very well
kept up.

She'd been expecting run down shacks made out of
metal and old boards like the ones she'd seen in National
Geographic, but they weren't like that at all. They were all
relatively new buildings, with tile roofs and stucco sides,
and the stucco looked freshly painted.

Around the village she'd seen small homes, and as they
drove down one of the small streets, she looked at them with
interest.

They were certainly very small and looked like they
were only one or two-bedroom buildings at the most, but
again each was relatively new, the stucco on them also
looked freshly painted, and each was surrounded with a
brightly painted fenced garden, each fence painted a
different bright color.

Beside many of the houses she could see small vegetable

gardens, and in one of the gardens an older lady was busy hanging out laundry on a line, her head wrapped in a bright colorful scarf, a large wicker basket filled with fresh washing standing next to her.

On the road there were several small children playing, and as Bernard maneuvered expertly around them, he waved and called out to them and they waved back, greeting him with happy, cheerful smiles.

In one of the gardens an older teenager, looking to be about eighteen or nineteen, was busy chopping wood, a small pile already lying by his side.

His chest was bare, and she could see sweat dripping down his face, but he seemed happy enough to just concentrate on his task, and seeing them drive up, he stopped, and grinned.

As he drove up and parked the jeep beside the house, Bernard turned to her.

"Wait here. I won't be long. Just have to have a word with Saul."

Then he jumped out of the jeep, and walking up the path to the door, turned to the boy, grinning.

"Hey, Mateo. How's it hanging?" the boy grinned back at him.

"Pointing up man. Pointing up."

"Great. Keep up the good work." Bernard said to him, laughing, "but don't overdo it Man. You don't want to wear it out."

Then he knocked on the door, and without waiting for anyone to answer, walked in.

What the hell were they talking about?

She'd never heard anything like it before and it was all Greek to her.

It's obviously some form of communication, she thought, but what kind, she had no clue.

Not that it matters, she thought to herself with resignation. *It's probably some kind of local dialect,* but since she'd probably never see this kid again, she didn't really care.

But as she watched him go back to his chopping, she thought again how interesting it was to see the comfortable manner Bernard had with all the natives, and especially how comfortable they all seemed to be with him.

Alina sat back in her seat and closed her eyes.

It was hot, but the sun was still low, and here the palm trees by the road sheltered her, and it was very comfortable just sitting here, relaxing.

After a couple of minutes, she heard the door open, and Bernard walked out with a tall, heavy set older man. They shook hands, the man grinned and patted his shoulder, then he walked back into his house, closing his door behind him as Bernard made his way back to the car.

Turning once more to the boy, he smiled at him.

"Take care of your old man dude." He said to him smiling. "Don't let him overdo it."

"Don't worry Bear." The kid answered grinning. "I got it covered."

Then he returned to his work while Bernard walk back to the car and getting in, started up the engine and drove them back through the village.

He made several more stops, greeting all the people he talked to cheerfully, and they all seemed happy to see him. Then finally getting into the car again he turned and looked at her, smiling.

"Sorry about that." He said. "Just had to take care of some business. Hope you weren't too bored."

"Oh no," she replied smiling back at him. "This is all very interesting. I'm glad I came with you today."

"So am I." He said, looking into her eyes, his gaze softening as he looked at her. Then after a moment his manner changed.

Smiling at her cheerfully now, he added,

"Only one more stop. There are some people I want you to meet. Jimena's making tea for us. I think you'll like them."

Then turning his gaze with determination to the road ahead, he drove them out of the village and back into the jungle.

After another half hour, he stopped in front of a bungalow set in a large garden.

It was across the road from a little beach, and the house was larger than the others had been in the village, but not by much.

There was a large vegetable garden by the side, and on the other side of it a young boy was playing on the grass, kicking a ball around.

As they drove up, the door opened, and a beautiful dark-haired woman stood in the doorway, smiling at them.

She looked to be in her late twenties, and she was dressed in the same kind of colorful cotton skirt and top all the local women seemed to wear here, but she certainly stood out, Alina thought.

As she stood there waiting for them, a tall heavy-set man walked up behind her, putting his hand on her shoulder, his gaze fixed towards their car.

Watching them make their way up the path, he smiled at Bernard once he reached the door and the two men hugged each other, obviously good friends.

Bernard bent and kissed the woman on the cheek, then turning to Alina, he smiled.

"Jimena, this is Alina." He said, still smiling. "Alina meet Jimena. She's our teacher."

"Yeah, she certainly is." The tall man replied, looking at her lovingly. "She's forever teaching me."

Jimena poked him in the ribs, but Alina could see the love

that was so evident between them. Then looking at her, the man smiled.

"I'm Emanuel." He said, grinning at her. "The gardener."

"A bit more than the gardener." Bernard said, laughing. "He oversees the whole island for me when I'm not here."

Bernard just smiled.

"Well, let's not just stand here." Jimena said, smiling at Alina, then she turned to the boy who was still playing with his ball.

"Put that down Pedro." She said to him, "go find Chico. That dog better not be eating my lettuce again."

The boy looked at her grinning, then dropping his ball he disappeared around the side of the house.

As she walked in, Alina saw the house was very comfortably furnished.

Not expensively by any means, but they seemed to have everything they needed, including a large TV, some kind of gaming system that the boy obviously used, and in front of the window there was a small desk with a laptop on it.

There was also a large bookcase crammed with books, and Alexia looked at it with interest.

Obviously very intelligent people, she thought, but then Emanuel held an important position here on the island, and Jimena was a teacher, so it was only to be expected.

They walked through the room and out to a large kitchen.

This too was well furnished with new appliances. The

clean counters gleamed in the sunlight, and the red geraniums in their small pots that Jimena had placed on the windowsill added a touch of color to the clean white kitchen, as did the colorful dishtowels that were hanging by the sink.

Walking out the back door, Jimena led them to a large table surrounded by wooden chairs that was sheltered by a pergola.

The table was standing on a stone patio. The same stone that had been used at the house, Alina noted with interest.

Must be local, she thought, *Interesting.*

On the pergola above the table, a huge beautifully flowering vine weaved through the open beams, its massive branches twisting around the wood. It was covered with large green leaves and bright red flowers and perfumed the air around them as Jimena led them outside and told them to sit.

Then returning to the kitchen, she quickly hurried back with a large tray, depositing it in the middle of the table.

Bernard was obviously used to the routine, and he grabbed the stack of small dessert plates, handing them around while Jimena poured the tea. Looking at Alina once more she smiled.

"I just made a loaf of fresh banana bread. Help yourself." She said to her, handing her a cup of the tea.

As she took a slice and bit into it, Alina sighed.

Wow, this was bloody good!

She'd had banana bread before, but none like this. When she complimented Jimena, she just smiled at her happily.

"It's the walnuts that really make it," she said. "We have a walnut tree in the garden."

"Yeah," Pedro said, grinning happily, his mouth full of banana bread. "And I get to pick the nuts."

There was a little dog tied to the side of the pergola, and it looked at them all quietly, wagging its tail.

This must be Chico. Alina thought, looking at it with a smile. *What a funny little dog!*

It was obviously a mongrel, of undetermined breed, it's white fur covered with patches of brown and black. Every once in a while, Pedro would throw it a piece of the bread, and the dog gulped it down greedily, looking up at him and wagging its tail, obviously wanting more.

Pedro had crawled up on Emanuel's lap while Jimena had been busy pouring the tea, and he sat there happily grinning at her, munching away on his bread, as Emanuel looked down at him with amusement, but behind the amusement she could see the love the man had for his son and it warmed her heart.

These were simple people, living a very simple life, but they were all very happy and content with what they had, because what they had was all they really needed.

When it really came down to it, Alina thought to herself, looking at them and smiling, but feeling a bit envious at the same time, *the love this family all so obviously felt for one another was all that really mattered in life.*

SEVEN

As they drove away Alina looked back, and she could see Pedro happily waving, his other hand firmly holding Chico by the collar while he wagged his tail and barked at the departing car.

That had definitely been different, she thought with a smile, but she'd really enjoyed meeting all of them.

Emanuel seemed like a very kind as well as very smart man, Jimena was beautiful and intelligent, and she'd enjoyed talking to her. She'd been very welcoming, making her feel very much at home with them, and Pedro .... Well, Pedro was just a joy.

She'd never seen such a well-adjusted happy boy.

He didn't have anywhere as much as most American children, yet in a lot of ways he seemed much happier.

Turning back to Bernard she looked at him and smiled.

. . .

"That was really great. They seem to be very nice people. I'm glad you took me to meet them."

He was concentrating on the road since it was full of ruts, but he smiled.

"Good." He said. "I thought you'd like them."

"So, where are we going next?" she asked him.

He turned to her.

"Time for us to have that swim." He said, and his eyes were twinkling again.

"It's bloody hot. You need to get rid of some of those clothes you're wearing. Just so you're more comfortable." He added, but he was grinning.

Alina could feel those tingles starting again.

When he said things like that he really got to her, and by the way he looked at her, he bloody well knew it. But she had to admit she was looking forward to that swim.

He was right. It was definitely bloody hot.

* * * *

They drove through the jungle for about fifteen minutes, and as he expertly maneuvered down the road, which was really more of a cart track than a road, she could see why he needed the jeep.

None of the roads on this island were very good, but he'd told her they weren't a priority. Everyone managed somehow, and there were more important things to concentrate their energies on.

. . .

As he turned off the road and parked the car in a small clearing, she looked around.

This was where they were going to swim?

It just looked like more jungle to her, but then what did she know.

He came around and helped her out of the car, then closing the door firmly behind her, grabbed a couple of towels and a blanket out of the back, and led her down a trail that led into the jungle.

It wasn't very wide, and was partially overgrown, but it was still navigable, and after a few minutes when she was beginning to wonder where the hell he was taking them, it suddenly ended, and she found herself in another clearing.

But this time it was at the side of a small pond.

It was very small, only about the size of a couple of swimming pools, but it was situated by the side of a cliff face, and as she looked up from the trail she gasped.

This was beautiful!

The pond was surrounded by flowering shrubs, obviously wild, but still very beautiful, and where the cliff rose out of the water, there was a small waterfall, the water making its way gradually from the top, over the rugged rocks on the cliff face into the pond, where it created large ripples on the otherwise smooth surface.

"Wow!" she said, truly impressed. "This is gorgeous!'

"Yes," he said smiling, "It's on my personal property as well, so we don't have to worry about being disturbed. There's a big pond near the village where all the kids swim, but this .... This is just for us to enjoy."

Bernard was already taking off his T-shirt and she followed his lead.

"I assume you can swim?" he asked, unsure now.

"I guess I should have asked before. I just never considered that maybe you couldn't."

"Yes, of course." She answered, smiling. She was just wearing her bikini now and he was looking at her admiringly.

"You look amazing in that thing Ally." He said grinning, "but I guess we should concentrate on why we're here." Then getting serious he looked at her.

"Be careful, okay? It's a bit deep, and there are rocks. It's not a swimming pool."

Smiling again, he grabbed her hand and dragged her into the water.

They swam and splashed around for about ten minutes, and as he took her hand once more and led her back out, Alina had to admit the water had been very refreshing. Just what they'd needed.

* * * *

As they made their way back over the soft grass to

where he'd spread the blanket he'd brought with them, his fingers softly caressed her hand, and she could feel the mood between them was slowly changing.

It was very beautiful here, very quiet, and very private.

They were both wet now, the water still dripping down their bodies, and handing her one of the towels he'd brought with them, he stood back from her, his eyes searching her face.

Where a few minutes ago they'd been laughing and playing in the water, now they were both standing completely still, just a few feet away from each other, just standing and looking at each other, and the air between them was filled with electricity.

Standing facing her, still looking at her, he slowly removed his swim trunks and began to dry himself, his eyes daring her to do the same.

Looking back at him she knew it was time.

It was time to stop fighting him. To give in to what she really wanted. What they both wanted.

Slowly she took off her bikini, and naked now as well, she started to dry herself with the towel, looking back at him while she rubbed her skin.

She could see his eyes changing, growing even darker as he looked at her, and finally throwing his towel down on the grass, he walked towards her.

With two steps he'd crossed the few feet of grass that lay

between them, and taking her towel from her hand, he looked deeply into her eyes.

"Here, let me help you." He said quietly, then moving even closer to her, he slowly began to wipe the water from her skin, looking at her body while he made his way down from her shoulders, caressing each part of it with the towel while he softly wiped.

God, that feels so good, she thought, finding it harder and harder to keep standing.

As he reached her breasts he looked at her face, and seeing she was enjoying his caress, he continued, looking down at her breasts as he softly rubbed her skin.

As his hand reached her nipples he abandoned the towel all together, rubbing them gently with his fingers, then lowering his head, he licked them, and she saw him look up and smile as he watched them harden with the touch of his tongue.

Obviously finding it too much, he caught his breath and groaned. No longer wanting to just play, he put his arms around her, drawing her closer to him, and kissed her passionately until they were both trembling with desire.

Pulling her down with him, he lay her gently on the rug, then laying down beside her, his hands roamed her body, caressing, exploring.

All the while he continued to kiss her, his breathing getting more and more heavy and labored.

. . .

The earth was soft, the grass was thick, and the rug made a very comfortable bed.

She put her arms around his neck, no longer objecting to his attentions, allowing him to do what he wanted and kissing him back each time his lips met hers. They were both naked and she could feel him getting harder, his erection straining against her body. After another few minutes he groaned.

"Shit. This is too hard Ally," he whispered, "I don't know how much longer I can restrain myself."

"So, don't." she answered."

As he lifted his head and looked at her questioningly, she looked back at him.

"Don't restrain yourself Bernard. Don't."

"You're sure?" he asked, looking back seriously at her. "You sure you want this Ally? Because once I start making love to you, I won't be able to stop."

"I'm sure. I tried, but I just can't fight this any longer. I want you," She said softly, looking up at him, "just as much as you want me."

He smiled then and kissed her again. Sitting up he looked down at her. "Don't you dare move." He said, and as she watched him, he reached into his shorts pocket and pulled out a condom.

"You know I've been with a lot of women Ally." He said, still speaking quietly, and looking at her seriously now.

"There's no point pretending I haven't, but I'm always careful. I always use protection. With you, I probably don't need to use this, but I want *you* to feel safe."

After he'd put it on he turned to her again.

"When I make love to you I don't want you worrying. I only want you thinking about one thing .... Me. And what I'm doing to you."

His eyes filled with lust, he slowly started to kiss her breasts, and she could feel his erection was getting larger as it strained against her.

After a minute, he moved his hand between her legs, and finding the most sensitive part of her, he gently rubbed.

She could feel herself coming, and her eyes closing, she felt him move over her and start guiding himself into her.

Fuck! She thought. *He wasn't exaggerating.*

He was huge, much bigger than any man she'd ever slept with before, and as he pushed himself into her and she felt herself stretching for him, she started coming again.

This time her orgasm was stronger than anything she could ever remember feeling.

It was so strong she could feel herself shaking as he kissed her, holding her gently in his arms.

"God, you're so gorgeous when you're coming." He murmured.

Slowly pulling out of her, he turned his attention once more to her breasts, taking each nipple into his mouth, licking it, and then biting it, as she moaned again.

After a minute she felt him thrust into her again, and again she started to come.

The sensations were getting stronger each time, and as she lay gasping in his arms, he pulled out again before he came. He gave her a few moments to recover, softly kissing her neck as her body slowly returned to normal, then she felt him pushing into her once more.

"Oh God. No. Please. I can't take much more."

"One more time Ally." He murmured. "Just one more time."

Then he rammed into her, hard this time, and as she felt him fill her completely, felt him rubbing against all the most sensitive parts of her, she felt her world start to explode around her.

She was floating, lost in a sea of pleasure, and as the feeling started to slowly subside, she felt him withdraw and then thrust into her once more.

Finally, having reached the end of his endurance, he came as well, and spent, he collapsed on the ground beside her, fighting to catch his breath.

. . .

"God, Ally, that was amazing." He said, when he was able to speak again, then turning to her, he smiled and stroked her cheek, his other arm around her still.

"That was fucking amazing."

"Yes, it was. "She agreed. She was still breathless, still finding it hard to talk.

He looked at her, his eyes soft with emotion.

"You sure made me wait for it." He said, smiling, "I'm not used to that, and it was bloody hard. I almost lost it a few times. You're so bloody hard to resist."

"The other night I was really tempted to follow you into your room. I was pretty sure you'd let me, but I could see you weren't really ready for me, so I made myself wait, and I tell you, walking away from you ... that was one of the hardest things I've ever had to do."

"But in the end, I'm glad I waited. I didn't just want one night with you. Just to scratch an itch. I wanted you to want me Ally. Really want me." He said, his eyes serious.

"It was bloody hard, but I knew it would be worth the wait, and I was right, God," he said with a happy sigh, "it was definitely worth it."

He pulled her closer to him, his eyes still looking at her tenderly, and stroking her face gently with his fingers, he bent his head, kissing her softly once more.

After a few minutes they both started to feel cold.

They were still wet from the water, and there was a cool

breeze softly blowing now. It had been a very hot day and the breeze was welcome, but it was definitely time to dress.

As she put her top and shorts back on, Alina smiled to herself.

Yes, this was definitely the right thing to do, she thought.

Making love with this man was bloody amazing. I'm not going to kid myself. I know it's just a bit of fun for him and that's how I'm going to look at it as well. Just a bit of fun. I certainly don't expect it to last.

But God, as he'd said, it had been fucking amazing.

It had definitely been the right decision, and she was going to make sure she enjoyed every minute of it while she could.

EIGHT

It didn't take him long to get them back home. The island, after all, wasn't that large.

Everything was just an hour away at most, and this was definitely a benefit, Alina thought. The island might be small, but when you wanted to reach any part of it you never had far to travel.

She'd been very glad to be able to sink into a bath and just relax.

It had been a very eventful day and it wasn't over yet. They still had dinner together, and he'd told her he'd ordered the musicians to play for them again, and he wanted her to wear one of the other dresses.

"You look amazing in that blue one," he'd said smiling, "but I'm sure you're getting sick of wearing it by now."

"Wear the white one tonight Ally. Dinner's at eight as usual. I'll come get you."

Then with a parting kiss he'd gone off to his office, leaving her to relax before they met again.

As she lay in her bath, Alina thought about their day. It had been an eye opener. In more ways than one.

She'd been surprised when she'd seeing how big he was.

When he'd told her about the Bear thing she'd figured he was just making it up to rile her.

She really hadn't expected it to be true, but it was definitely true, she thought, smiling to herself.

She had felt it for herself, and no doubt about it, making love to a man that large was definitely a different experience.

They said size didn't matter, that it was what the man did with what he had that made the difference, and in a lot of ways they were right.

The other men she'd slept with had definitely known how to use what they had, and she'd never had any reason to complain, but making love to him .... Well it had been fucking amazing, just like he'd said.

When he was inside her he totally filled her, and there wasn't a single part of her that was left untouched. He could make her come just by moving it.

She'd never come so much before in her life, and she wasn't all that sure that would be such a good thing in the long run.

. . .

She'd had to end up begging him to stop, it had all been so overwhelming.

Was it going to be like that every single time?

The thought both scared her and intrigued her, but she knew that now that she'd slept with him once she would continue sleeping with him as long as he wanted her. She was definitely under his spell, and she really had no choice.

Seeing him talking and laughing with the men who worked for him, joking with the kids, that had really surprised her as well. He had such a playboy image she really hadn't expected to see this caring side of him.

Yes, he was definitely a playboy, there was more than enough evidence of that, but nobody had shown this other side of him in any of the articles she'd read.

But he was also a lot more than people knew, and that was really too bad.

As she thought about it, Alina made up her mind.

Maybe it was time that somebody did something about that, and maybe she was the perfect person to do it. After all, she had the perfect opportunity.

The second part she'd written, the part about his education, was good, she knew that. The fact that he was a Harvard graduate, had gone to business school and had an MBA was no small accomplishment, but it wasn't, after all, something new.

It had been mentioned in articles about him before.

. . .

But the way he lived here on this island, the way he cared for the people who depended on him here, that was new.

It should be out there as well, and weren't they after all his PR firm?

Wasn't it up to them to help him create a positive image?

Well, this was a major side of him, a side that almost nobody knew about, and it should be out there just as prominently as the playboy side.

For many people his womanizing ways were what they found the most fascinating, but there were many others who would find it much more interesting to know that behind that charming woman-eater exterior there was also a real man.

A man who was worthy of respect.

While she lay back thinking about it, she realized that this was true for her as well.

Slowly, seeing him here on this island that was his home, her image of him had changed.

She'd been impressed by what she'd learned about him, and now she not only was incredibly attracted to him physically, she really did respect him as well.

God knows he isn't perfect, Alina thought.

She definitely wasn't fond of the way he went through women, and this irresponsible playboy image he seemed to be more than happy to portray had been more than enough to put her off, but now she also knew that was only one side of him, and when it came down to it, was that really the most important side?

The more she got to know him, the more she knew it wasn't.

He had a lot of good traits.

Traits that people should know about before they judged him, and she was determined to be the one to showcase them.

She'd keep the second part she'd already written, and when the rest of the article was finished, she'd give him both versions to read and let him choose which one he wanted printed.

It was after all his life and his decision, but she really hoped he would choose the one she was going to write the next day.

That was the real him and the world should know about it.

When she opened the door to him that evening, she could see the look of admiration in his eyes.

"Wow." He said softly, looking at her with appreciation. "You look stunning Alina. Just stunning. I thought the blue one would be my favorite, but this one .... This one really takes my breath away."

He bent down and softly kissed her cheek.

"I've chosen another piece from my grandmother's jewelry collection for you to wear tonight. This will be perfect." He said quietly, as he pulled a long box out of his tux pocket.

"There are no earrings to go with this, but you don't really need them."

He opened the box and she gasped. He was right. It was perfect.

The necklace was again very delicate and very simple. Just six diamonds set on a white gold chain, but the diamonds were much larger this time, and they sparkled in the hall light as she looked at them.

He put the box down on the small table outside her room, then holding the necklace in his fingers, he put it gently around her neck, turning her around to do up the clasp, his fingers stopping to caress her skin once he'd finished.

Walking her over to the mirror that hung on the other wall, he stood her in front of it, standing behind her.

"Look at yourself Ally." He said quietly, his voice husky now. "Look how beautiful you are."

She had to admit it really did look great, and as she looked at her reflection he bent down, kissing her neck."

"God, Ally." He whispered. "If those musicians weren't waiting for us I'd forget about dinner and just take you to my room. You have no idea how much seeing you looking like this makes me want you again."

. . .

H was looking at her in the mirror and smiling.

"But I need to restrain myself." He said.

"It's only a couple hours before you'll be back in my bed, and you need to build up your energy. You'll need it."

His smile turned wicked as he guided her once again down the stairs.

The dinner was wonderful as usual, and this time Edwardo greeted her just as he did Bernard, and she smiled at him.

After dinner he insisted they had to dance again, and as she waltzed again in his arms, he pressed her close and she could feel how much he wanted her.

After half an hour it had obviously become more than he could take. Walking her out, he turned to the men playing, and shook each of their hands.

"Thanks guys." He said grinning, "You're amazing as always."

"Our pleasure Bear." The leader of the group said, and they both hugged each other, then he turned back to her, and taking her by the hand again, led her purposefully back up the stairs.

This time, instead of heading for her room, he headed in the other direction. When she looked at him questioningly, he smiled at her.

"You're going to be sleeping with me from now on." He said. "You're not going to need that room any longer."

. . .

"Tomorrow Melinda will have your things moved into the Master Suite, but I have no intention of waiting that long. You're moving in right now.

This calls for a celebration, and I know just the way I want to celebrate."

They had reached the large double doors that led to his bedroom, and he looked at her with that sexy stare that had graced so many magazine covers.

As she looked back at him, she wondered at the amazing Fate that had led her to this place.

Here she was, with one of the sexiest men on earth, being led by him into his bedroom, and once again she felt those tingles she was getting to know so well running up and down her spine.

He was smiling softly at her, and lowering his head he kissed her, then holding her hand still firmly in his, he opened the door to the suite and led her inside.

Alina had travelled on business before. Because of her job she'd had the chance to meet a lot of wealthy people, had taken part in meetings in a lot of their luxurious suites, and was quite used to the opulent way in which they lived, but Bernard's suite still took her breath away.

As he opened the door and led her inside, she found herself in a large hallway.

There were double doors on each side of it, a beautiful

carved antique table on the far wall with an equally beautiful mirror hanging over it, and a huge crystal chandelier illuminated the whole space.

Opening the door on the right, he led her into what was obviously the living area.

Also decorated with beautiful dark antique furniture, it was filled with plush maroon couches, brocade chairs, and oriental rugs. On the walls hung what looked to her inexperienced eye to be original paintings, painted in the same style she knew Matisse and Van Gough had used.

These surely couldn't be originals she thought, *but with this man? Who knew.*

There was a small bar on the far side of the room, and he walked towards it, picking up a bottle of cognac and pouring some of it into two brandy snifters that were standing conveniently next to it.

Handing her one, he put his arm around her and guided her over to the French doors on the far side of the room.

As he walked with her through the doors, she found herself on a small stone patio, overlooking the ocean.

It was just below them, and even though it was now quite dark, she could hear the waves crashing on the rocks.

The breeze had picked up, and as she looked out she could see the outline of several palm trees on each side of the terrace, their huge fronds blowing in the wind.

It was still very warm, and the breeze felt cool on her skin as she stood there looking out, sipping her cognac. He was standing very close, his arm around her, his fingers softly caressing her shoulders.

"I hoped you enjoyed our evening." He said, smiling at her. "Personally, I was looking forward more to the next part."

He took a sip of his Cognac, then he put it down on the table next to him, and, reaching over he took her glass out of her hand, putting it down next to his.

"I think it's time I showed you the rest of the suite." He said, and his eyes twinkled as he smiled at her again.

They walked back into the hall, and as he opened the other door, Alina could see that the bedroom was almost as big as the living area.

It was absolutely huge.

There was a fireplace, a seating area in front of it, and there were also French doors here leading out to the same patio, but what really caught her eye was the bed on the far wall, facing out onto the water.

Made of dark wood, the exquisitely carved headboard loomed over the king-size bed.

The bed itself was covered with a beautiful hand-made cream-colored quilt, and it had already been turned down for them, letting her see the crisp white linen sheets and pillowcases, each trimmed with what looked like hand-made lace.

Amazing, Alina thought to herself, and as she stood there looking at it, he came up quietly behind her, and slowly removed the necklace. Then placing it in the case he'd laid on the dresser, he turned back to her, and kissing her, he unzipped her dress.

"I've enjoyed seeing you wear this Love." He whispered, "You looked amazing tonight, but for what I have in mind next, you're not going to need it."

He made love to her for what seemed like hours that night, and after she'd come for the fourth time, she finally had to beg him again to stop.

After he'd lay back on his pillow, spent, he'd turned to her and laughed.

"I was easy on you today," he said, his eyes twinkling as they sparkled in the moonlight, "but four times? That's not nearly enough. I'm going to expect more from you Ally, much more."

"What you need is a lot more practice, and hard as it will be, I can see it will be up to me to make sure you get it." Then cupping her body against his, he whispered into her ear.

"Now get some sleep. We'll try it again in the morning. Don't worry Love. I'll make sure you do it until you get this right."

She heard him softly laugh as he put his arms around her and drew the covers over them both.

NINE

She woke to the feel of his lips on her neck as he softly kissed her. His body cupping hers, she could feel how aroused he was again, and as he turned her towards him she shivered in anticipation.

Had he really meant what he'd said?

Was he going to expect her to have more orgasms?

Surely, he'd been kidding.

Yes, she'd heard of women who had as many as twenty at a time, but she was sure they were very extreme cases.

She'd discussed this with some of her girlfriends and none of them had managed more than four, and those had been exceptional. Usually one or two seemed to be the norm and most men were very happy if you even had one.

He was kissing her neck softly now, and when he looked at her she saw that hungry look in his eyes again. Pushing away the sheets, he leaned over her, licking her nipples, and as she closed her eyes she felt his hand making its way between her legs.

Finding what he was looking for he softly rubbed, then as she started to feel herself getting wet, he thrust into her, and, as before, she immediately started to come.

When she'd come four times she turned to him imploringly.

"No more, Bernard. Please. No more." She begged.

"Oh yes, love, I'm going to do it again. And you're going to enjoy it even more."

Then he pushed into her, filling her completely, and when she came she was shaking.

"Oh God, I can't." She whispered. "Bernard, please I can't!"

"Yes Love, you can." He said, his voice husky, and he thrust into her again, this time with full force.

Each time it was stronger than the time before, and each time she felt herself losing control more and more, and still he wouldn't stop.

He'd withdrawn again, still without coming, and as she lay in his arms, shaking, she begged him again.

"Please Bernard. Please. I can't do this again." He softly stroked her hair, watching her as she slowly caught her breath. When she'd almost recovered, he leaned over her again.

"You have no idea what you're capable off love, but don't worry. I'm going to show you."

Then he thrust into her, hard, and then started to move, and as she felt him inside her again, all her insides vibrating while he rubbed against her, she heard herself scream as the feeling started all over again.

"Oh God! Oh God!" she screamed, grabbing his shoulders for support.

This orgasm was so strong her whole body was shaking violently.

The pleasure she was feeling was more intense than anything she'd ever thought it possible to feel, and it went on for much longer than any orgasm had ever lasted before. It was so intense it was almost too much for her to stand.

As it finally dissipated after what seemed like an eternity, she slowly caught her breath again and, still panting, she opened her eyes.

He was looking at her, and he was grinning. When she looked at him, alarmed, he softly stroked her face, still grinning.

"Don't worry. I came that time. You were way too out of it to notice. Now that, that's the way to have a proper orgasm." He said, his grin even wider than before.

"They should all be like that." Then his eyes softened as he continued to look at her.

"I could see that was enough for now. You're not used to this yet and I don't want you to get sore. You've got to build up gradually."

"But you managed to come seven times this time Ally,

and that last time, watching you, that was fucking awesome. I almost came again it was so incredible."

He leaned over her, kissing her neck again.

"God, you're so amazing. I can't wait to see you do that again." Then looking up and seeing the alarmed expression on her face, he laughed.

"Don't worry. You'll have all day to recover. We won't try it again until tonight. Then we'll try for ten."

She looked back at him in horror.

Was this man crazy?

Ten?

Was he trying to kill her?

He was still smiling, and obviously very amused.

"In a lot of ways, you're such a little innocent." He said, laughing. "You really have no idea what you're capable of."

"Look what you did this morning. Did you ever think you'd manage seven orgasms in a row?"

"No." She said, quietly, "But Bernard, ten? That's impossible!"

"No Love, it isn't." He said. "You'll do it for me. And very soon." Then still looking at her, he sighed.

"And why the hell are you still calling me Bernard?

Nobody calls me that. Why aren't you calling me Bear

like everyone else?" then suddenly understanding, he laughed.

"It's what I said before isn't it. Don't take that seriously Love." He said, still laughing,
    "I told you. I was just trying to rile you up. Yeah, it's true, the guys kid me about it sometimes, but that's not really why everyone calls me Bear."
    He sat up then, leaning against the pillows, and she sat up next to him.

"It's mainly because I made most of my money in the Bear market." He said.
    When she looked at him, uncomprehendingly, he patiently explained.

"A Bear market is when stocks are falling. People get scared and they sell, a lot of times way under value. If you're smart and you can afford it, that's when you should buy not sell. If you buy wisely, you can make a lot of money, which is exactly what I did."
    Turning to her, he stroked her face and looked at her seriously.
    "That's really why I ended up with that nickname. So now that you know the truth will you please call me Bear?" Looking at her wickedly again he laughed.

"I think we know each other intimately enough to relax the formalities, don't you?"

Alexia sighed, then looked up at him and smiled.

"Yes, I guess so .... Bear." She added, and he smiled back at her.

"There you go. That wasn't hard, was it? Any more than it was to have seven orgasms." He added, grinning wickedly again.

"You'll manage ten for me tonight Love, and you'll enjoy them even more than you did this morning. You'll see." He said softly, and as she looked up at him in horror, he was still grinning as he bent his head and kissed her again.

Suddenly there was a knock on the bedroom door and a cheerful female voice called out.

"Mr. Bear, you up Mr. Bear? Breakfast is out on the patio. Now get your ass out of bed or the coffee will get cold." As Alina looked at the door in shock, Bear laughed.

"Thanks Melinda," he said, still laughing. "I'm getting my ass out of bed right now."

"Bloody time." Alina heard her mutter, then she heard her footsteps receding down the hall.

Still Laughing, Bear got out of bed, and looked at her.

"Melinda takes a bit of getting used to, but she has a heart of gold." Then he pointed to the closed door on her side of the room.

"There's your bathroom. You'll find a clean robe in

there. There are some new toothbrushes as well in one of the drawers. Meet you out on the terrace. And hurry up or the coffee will be cold." Grinning again, he added,

"Now get your ass out of bed Love. It will be back in there again soon enough, I'll see to that."

Still grinning, he opened the door on his side which she assumed led to his bathroom and disappeared from view.

This whole thing is going to take some getting used to. She thought to herself with a sigh, then following his command she got up.

TEN

As she stepped out onto the patio Alina could see that it was yet another beautiful day.

There seemed to be nothing but beautiful days here she thought. He'd told her that they frequently had storms and they could be pretty bad, but on a day like today it was hard to believe.

He was sitting in his robe, texting on his phone and he smiled at her when she walked out. Sitting down she poured herself a cup of the still hot coffee and prepared to wait.

He was concentrating on what he was doing now, and since it was obviously important, she was quite content to just sit there silently and enjoy the view.

This was certainly a hell of a way to wake up.

Finishing what he was doing, he closed his phone and

placing it on the table beside him he smiled at her as he took a sip of his coffee.

"So, writing again today?" he asked.

"Yes," she replied, smiling back at him. "I want to get this article written and I've got an idea I want to work on while it's still fresh in my mind." He just smiled but he didn't reply. Then after a minute he turned to her.

"I'm going to be busy most of today and tomorrow with island business. I know you still have questions to ask me. Can we do it after that?

I promise to give you all the time you need then, but right now there are a few things that I really need to look after."

"Problems?" she asked, cautiously. She didn't want to pry, but she was definitely curious.

"Yeah, sort of." He said sighing.

"Jimena is our only teacher right now. When I first hired her five years ago that worked out well. There weren't that many school age kids here, but as you know, kids grow." He said, sighing again.

"We've got twenty more now and it's really too much for her to handle. There's a young girl I'm putting through teacher's college and she'll be qualified next year, but meanwhile I need someone to fill in the gap and that's not easy to find."

. . .

He turned to her and smiled.

"But I'll do it. I'm sure there is someone out there and if there is I'll find her.

These kids need proper schooling if they're ever going to get anywhere in life and I'm determined to see they get it."

Alina looked at him in amazement. He took care of educating them as well?

Was there no limit to what this man did?

"I'm sure you will." She replied. "Are you this involved in everything that goes on here?"

"Of course." He answered, surprised by her question. "I own this island. These people depend on me. It's a responsibility I don't take lightly."

Then sighing again, he added,

"They had enough of that with the previous owner."

"Really?" Alina asked curiously. "Who was the previous owner? What was he like?"

"He was a South American from a rich family and he really didn't give a damn about this place."

"I first came here with the Peace Corp when I was a student. I worked here for three weeks and the conditions these people had to endure were totally disgusting.

There was no doctor, no school, very little food, and they lived in shacks with dirt floors.

That man was filthy rich, yet all he used this place for was as a party place."

He looked angry and disgusted now as he continued.

"I vowed that one day when I'd made enough money I'd come back and help them. Thankfully when this island came for sale I could afford to buy it, and slowly, over the eight years I've owned it I've managed to do a lot."

"I had proper homes built for them first off. Nobody should have to live the way they did. Then gradually we built the school, the clinic, got a doctor to live here full time. I've even sent one of our oldest boys to medical school."

Bear smiled then.

"Sebastian's smart as a whip. He's doing his internship in Miami now." Then he looked at her, still smiling.

"But I'm sure none of this interests you." He said.

"Your wrong." Alina replied. "It interests me very much."

As she settled down in the library to work, she thought about what she'd learned from him at breakfast.

Would this man ever stop surprising her?

Now she was even more sure that changing the article was the right thing to do.

People needed to know about this.

He was really an amazing man and people needed to know the real him.

After lunch she'd finished her first draft and was feeling very good about it. It had turned out really well.

It was another hot day and she decided to take a break and go sit out on the patio and read for a bit. It had been a busy few days and she could do with some down time.

Grabbing her novel from her purse, she walked outside, marveling yet again at how beautiful it was here.

I could get used to this, she thought. *Not that I'd ever get the chance.*

Refusing to think about where that had come from, she banned the thought out of her mind and settled down in a chair to read.

After half an hour she was starting to get thirsty. Getting up she walked around the side of the patio.

Hadn't Bear said the kitchen was here somewhere? Maybe she could get a drink there.

As she turned the corner and walked further along the patio, she heard voices coming from the open windows just in front of her.

She realized it was Bear, and he sounded very angry. Curious now, she walked closer.

She didn't really mean to listen in to his conversation, but he was speaking very loudly and here in these normally quiet surroundings, his voice carried.

Very curious now, she stood and listened.

"Don't fuck with me." She heard him say, and his voice was nothing like she'd ever heard him use before.

She knew him as a playboy, a philanthropist, and she'd known he was a businessman, but she'd never really seen this side of him before.

"Don't fuck with me Gorgio." She heard him say again.

"You know what will happen. Do the job I'm paying you to do and I will treat you fairly, but if I find you're trying to screw me, I'll crush you, and you know that's not an idle threat. I've done it before. You've seen it for yourself. You don't want to end up like Kane."

As she stood there listening, the way he spoke, the total coldness in his voice, made her shiver.

He sounded totally ruthless, and when he was like this he was damn scary.

As she silently backed away, retracing her steps, she marveled yet again at the complexity of this man's character.

One minute he was loving and caring the other he was cold and ruthless.

As a successful businessman I suppose he has to be tough, Alina thought as she made her way back into the library, *but this had been more than tough.*

The man she'd just heard was cold, heartless and talked about crushing people as if it was an everyday occurrence.

How could a man have two such completely different sides to his personality?

During the day while she'd been working, Melinda had moved all her things just like Bear had said she would, and when she walked back into the master bedroom and into her bathroom she saw the walk-in closet next to it contained all her clothes now, all neatly hung and put away.

The closet was huge, and her few things looked lost in it she thought, *but then everything about this place was huge, including the man who owned it.*

As she lay in her bath and thought about what she'd found out that day, she marveled at what a complex character he was.

He was obviously a ruthless businessman, but he was also caring and thoughtful when it came to this island, and he took his obligations to the people here very seriously.

She couldn't believe how seriously.

There was certainly much more depth to this man than she'd ever suspected.

On the other hand, he certainly lived very well, enjoyed all the good things in life, and felt no qualms about filling his obviously ferocious sexual appetite.

Take this orgasm thing.

Wasn't this a bit obsessive?

She could see him getting turned on by the woman he was with having one. Most guys did, but wasn't he pushing it a bit far?

Though he certainly seemed to know what he was talking about in that department. She had to admit she'd surprised herself this morning.

Seven orgasms? Who would have believed it?

She certainly wouldn't have a week ago, but with Bear she was quickly finding out that just about anything was possible.

He'd told her he expected her to have ten that night, and after this morning she knew he meant it, and the thought scared her, but she had to admit it intrigued her as well.

He definitely seemed to know what he was doing, though going on how much experience he'd had she wasn't surprised, but expecting her to have ten orgasms? It sounded a bit much to her.

Surprisingly though, as she thought about it, she found she was actually curious to see if she could do it.

She had to admit that even though it had scared her because she'd never done anything like that before, she'd enjoyed this morning, and that last orgasm ... that had been amazing.

Could she do it again?

It was still a bit scary, but she was also curious now to find out if she could.

ELEVEN

He'd told her to wear the third dress tonight, so that's what she did.

It was a deep burgundy red, and where the blue one had shown off her eyes and the white one had made her look very elegant, this one made her look very sexy and a bit slutty at the same time, like a woman of the world.

Which is how I'm starting to feel these days, she thought to herself smiling.

A woman with an internationally famous lover who has seven orgasms in one session? That sounded pretty worldly to her.

When she walked back into the bedroom he was already there, dressed in his tux and putting on his cufflinks. He turned to her, and as he looked at her he smiled.

"Every time you wear something new you amaze me Love." He said,

"This one makes you look just as beautiful as you did in the other two."

Looking lecherously at her, he added quietly,

"And very fuckable. It's definitely a turn-on that dress."

Reaching into the small jewelry case that lay open on the dresser next to him, he took out another exquisitely beautiful but simple necklace.

This was just a pendant on a gold chain. The pendant was a large ruby and it was surrounded by small perfect diamonds.

As he fastened the clasp he bent down and kissed her neck, then grabbing her hand he led her out the door.

As they walked towards the stairs, he looked at her again with that famous stare.

"We're going to have a quick dinner tonight Love." He said quietly, looking at her with those deep dark eyes, "I want to get us back here as soon as possible so we can start on the next part of the evening."

Still staring at her he added." I've been looking forward to this all day."

As he guided her out to the terrace Alina started to feel those tingles again.

She'd been thinking about it herself but hearing him say it .... That was starting to make her feel nervous.

She might look worldly, but right now she didn't feel very worldly at all.

* * * *

True to his word Bear didn't linger and an hour later they were walking back into the bedroom.

As soon as he walked in the door he took of her necklace, then immediately unzipped her dress, and slipping it off left it lying on the ground at her feet while he took of her underwear.

Naked now he lay her on the bed and standing over her, he took off his own clothes. Then grabbing a condom from his bedside drawer, he quickly put it on and lay down beside her.

"Now, where were we?" he murmured, as he kissed her neck again, his hands on her breasts.

Half an hour later she'd come six times.

Tonight, she found the first few were still good, but nothing to write home about compared to what she now knew would follow. As they had slowly gotten stronger and stronger she'd found herself looking forward with anticipation.

Could she do this?

Bear was really taking his time, letting her recover completely before making her come again, but as her orgasms got stronger and stronger, she found they lasted longer as well.

The next one was really strong, and she was panting when she finally opened her eyes.

He seemed to be in a much different mood tonight. As she looked at him he just looked back at her hungrily, then pushing into her again he bent his head and bit her neck.

As she felt him move inside her she felt herself coming again and this time it was even stronger than it had been that morning.

As she felt the sensations slowly start to diminish she opened her eyes to see him still looking at her with that now famous stare, and it sent cold shivers down her back.

This man wasn't playing around tonight. He was deadly serious here.

"Now we're getting to the good part." He said, his voice husky, and this time, before she'd fully recovered, he thrust into her again.

"Oh God, Bear," she cried as she felt herself losing control.

She was starting to shake again, and the feeling was starting to get unbearable.

When she finally stopped shaking and opened her eyes, he was still staring at her, his eyes both hungry and determined. He leaned over her, biting her neck again, and again, before she knew it, he was inside her and she was coming again.

She was losing all control now.

The sensations were so strong they were taking over. She found herself riding the waves of pleasure, never wanting them to stop.

As she finally felt them subside, she opened her eyes again, still gasping, and found he was staring at her again, then slowly he smiled, a soft, knowing smile, his eyes staring deeply into hers.

He didn't say a word, just bent and kissed her neck softly, then lifting his head again, he suddenly rammed into her with full force, filling her so completely she felt like he was going to split her in two.

As her world once again began to spin around her, her body shook with a feeling so strong it almost overwhelmed her. Grabbing his shoulders again she screamed.

"Oh God. Bear. Please!"

"Once more." she heard him say, his voice now gruff and determined, and while she was still reacting to the first one, he pulled out and rammed into her again, and she felt another orgasm starting.

He hadn't given her any time.

She was still coming, but he was already moving inside her, and her body still welcome him, still wanted more.

. . .

The feelings he was creating within her were now twice as powerful, twice as strong as wave after wave of pleasure rolled over her.

"Oh God. Bear. Oh God." She cried, as she felt herself losing all control. Then all she could do was feel.

When she finally opened her eyes, he was looking at her, and as she looked back at him he softly stroked her face. He wasn't smiling or grinning now, and his eyes were serious.

"That was the most beautiful thing I've ever seen." He said. "You're amazing Ally," he said quietly. "I could get addicted to this." Then his mood changed again.

"That was eleven." He said, grinning wickedly, "That last one was a double one, so twelve really. I wanted to see if you could handle it, and you were amazing.

You're ready for the final push now."

She looked at him with alarm.

The final push? What the hell was that?

Seeing how anxious she looked, he smiled, stroking her face again.

"I could tell you were a very sensual woman when I first met you Ally." He said quietly,

"That's something you can see right away, but you amazed me once I found out just how really sensual you are. I think tomorrow you'll amaze yourself."

"Tomorrow?" she asked him nervously, "You want me to do this again tomorrow?"

"No Love." He said, "Not this. This was just practice. Just getting you ready.

Tomorrow I'm going to push you to the limit." He said, still smiling at her.

S

he was starting to get scared now.

This was getting crazy.

As he saw the fear in her eyes, he stroked her face softly again.

"There's nothing for you to be scared about Ally." He said quietly.

"I just want to see how much your body is willing to come for me. When it reaches its limit, it will let you know.

Your body isn't stupid. It won't let you do more than it can handle. I just want you to show me how much that is."

Holy Shit! Alina thought. *This is really pushing it.*

Can I do this?

He could tell what she was thinking now by her eyes, and again he smiled at her softly.

"Yes, you can do this. Don't you want to know yourself? Know how far your body will let you go to please me?"

bent down and kissed her softly.

"You're already pleasing me so much Ally. I want to know how much more you have to give me."

. . .

She had totally recovered now, and now that she could think straight again, she wondered how the hell their relationship had changed so much in just a few short days.

When she'd first come to this island with him she'd been sure he was an irresponsible playboy and the last person on earth she would ever fall for.

In fact, she'd laughed at Gerald for even suggesting that something like that could possibly happen.

Now here she was, prepared to sing his praises in the article she was writing about him, and what was even more disturbing, she was seriously considering pushing her body to its limits in order to please him.

How the hell had she fallen so completely under his spell?

TWELVE

She woke to the feel of his kisses on her neck, and immediately she felt herself stiffen.

Oh God! She thought. *I'm not ready for this!*

As he felt her resisting him, he slowly turned her around to face him.

"Don't fight me Love." He said quietly. "Don't be afraid. I'm not going to push you. Just let yourself go. Your body knows what it wants."

He softly stroked her face while he looked into her eyes.

"I want you so much it hurts. Let's just see where this goes."

She looked back at him.

She was scared. Really scared, but she couldn't say No to him.

Somehow, this man had gotten to her.

He was making her body go to places she'd never known it was possible for it to go, but much as it scared her, she couldn't turn him down, because now she wanted this just as much as he did.

Seeing she was still apprehensive, he took his time, kissing her, caressing her, making her want him so much, and slowly she found herself relaxing in his arms.

God! What he was doing felt so fucking good, she thought. She didn't want him to stop.

He was still kissing her, but he was teasing her now as well. As her body started to react to him, he would withdraw, never quite letting her go where she wanted to go.

His fingers played between her legs, but whenever she felt herself starting to come again, he would stop, until she felt like she could no longer stand it.

"

Oh God, Bear." She whimpered. "Don't stop. Please. Don't stop."

Seeing she was finally ready to succumb to him again, he moved over her, pushing himself into her, and she started to come, but this time he wasn't going to wait.

While her body was still vibrating with pleasure, he pulled out, then immediately rammed into her again, filling her completely, and her body started coming again, even stronger than before.

. . .

But still he wasn't done.

He didn't wait for her to finish.

As soon as she started to come down, even slightly, he pulled out and then thrust into her, and the feelings he was creating within her were so strong she could hardly stand it.

"Oh God! Bear." She screamed as she just kept coming over and over again.

It was one long incredible wave of pleasure and there was no end. She was no longer aware of anything but her body and how incredible he was making her feel.

Every time she felt it was starting to subside, he rammed into her again, starting it all over again, not giving it time to stop. And each time the feelings were more powerful than the last, taking her far beyond anything she'd ever felt before.

Finally, after what seemed like forever, she felt herself slowly relaxing.

The feelings were slowly subsiding, but they had been so strong, so powerful, that once they finally stopped, her body started to shake uncontrollably.

She lay in his arms, and still shaking, she found herself whimpering, wanting more.

God! What was this man doing to her?

She'd never felt anything like this before.

This uncontrollable need to have him inside her was almost overpowering, and as she lay there, trying to calm herself down, she could feel that longing was still there.

. . .

Finally, as her body stopped shaking and her breathing returned to normal, she opened her eyes, and saw he was softly smiling.

"You're amazing Ally." He said softly, "Really amazing. The way your body reacts to me .... God, what a turn on you are! I could lay here fucking you all day." Then he looked at her seriously, searching her eyes.

"You were far from done you know that, don't you?" He said, stroking her face. "Even after I pulled out, even after your body stopped shaking, it still wanted me, didn't it?"

She looked up at him.

He knew, she thought, *He'd felt it for himself. How could she deny it?*

"Yes." She whispered. "I still wanted you."

He smiled then, and kissed her softly.

"You came twelve times, you know that? Twelve times one after another. It was mind blowing.

I was the one who finally couldn't stand it any longer." He got serious then and still looking at her, he searched her eyes.

"You have so much to give me Ally." He said quietly. "So much. And I want to experience it all.

I can see how much your body craves me now. It wants

me, and it wants to show me just how much. It's more than ready, and I can hardly wait." He whispered softly.

He was still holding her, still looking at her, when there was a knock on the door and his mood changed.

"Mr. Bear." She heard Melinda say. "Mr. Bear, are you up yet?

Are you going to stay in that bloody bed forever? I don't have all day. And you don't either.

The coffee's on the terrace. Get up and make some money, you lazy bastard. The bills won't pay themselves."

Then muttering to herself, she walked away.

Bear turned to her, his eyes twinkling.

"I guess that means we'd better get out of here." Then his face got serious again, and he took her hand and kissed it, his eyes still on her face.

"You're a dream come true Love." He said softly, "I can hardly wait to see what you'll do for me tonight." Then he got up and giving her one last smile, disappeared into his bathroom.

As she sat in the library that morning, she slowly sipped her coffee, still thinking about what had just happened.

What the hell was happening to her?

He was turning her into a woman she no longer knew. Who was this wanton creature she'd become?

This woman who wanted this man so shamelessly?

Who was obviously willing to push herself to whatever extremes he demanded of her to please him?

And how the hell had it happened in just these few short days?

She was looking forward to tonight just as much as he was. Wanted to see what he would do next to her and how much more her body could take.

Even now, sitting here dressed and ready to work, she could still feel that longing deep inside her. It never went away now, and it was bloody scary.

Where the hell was all this going to lead?

She was really scared to find out, knew that if she was smart she'd put a stop to this before it went any further, but she also knew that it was too late.

She couldn't resist him now.

She wanted him just as much as he wanted her, and the thought of what would happen when she had to leave, when it was over, when she could no longer sleep with him again, was too scary to think about.

She was hooked, addicted to him, and she couldn't do a bloody thing about it.

Sighing, she turned to her laptop and opened it.

Bear had told her he would be busy most of the day. It was much too good an opportunity for her to pass up.

Regardless of what was happening between them, she still had a job to do.

She'd come here to write this article on him and she was determined to do a good job of it.

Putting aside all her personal feelings, she knew that what she'd found out about this man the last few days was too good just to dismiss. It needed to be out there, for people to read.

He wasn't perfect by any means.

There were a lot of things about him she didn't like, would never like, but he had so many good and admirable qualities that needed to be heralded, and she was determined to make sure they were.

THIRTEEN

She hadn't seen him all day and it had worked out very well Alina thought to herself.

She'd been able to concentrate on her work, and the article she was writing was going to be amazing. One of the best things she'd ever written in fact, she was sure of it.

She'd finished the second part and she was very pleased with it.

She'd managed to put in all about his island and the work he did here, and she knew as she read it over that it said exactly what she'd wanted it to say.

People knew he was a playboy and that would never change. He was constantly giving them more and more evidence of that, but once they read this they would also know there was a serious, caring and compassionate side to him.

. . .

Smiling to herself Alina finished her tea and packed up her notes. She'd go up and have a nice relaxing soak then she would get ready for dinner.

Since he hadn't told her to wear anything in particular, she'd just choose one of the dresses that already hung in her closet. Still smiling, she walked slowly out of the library and up the stairs.

As she opened the door to the bedroom she noticed the dress on the bed. He'd obviously had another one delivered for her to wear tonight. This one was completely different from any of the others.

It was just a short simple black dress made completely out of lace. See-through lace, and it wasn't lined.

There were black feathers on the top and a row on the bottom which she was sure would give her some coverage, but no a hell of a lot.

Next to it was another underwear bag and a pair of very thin black strapped sandals with four inch heels.

The only thing the underwear bag contained was a pair of black stockings. They were the kind that didn't need anything to hold them up since they had a stretchy top.

Just stockings? No underwear? She thought, *What the hell?*

But looking at the dress, she could see why. It was so see through that one really couldn't wear any underwear with it.

. . .

As she put it on after her bath, Alina saw that the feathers were very strategically placed. Looking in the mirror she could see that they covered her nipples and her pubic area, but not much else. She was just as exposed as she would have been in a bikini.

The dress was skin-tight and very, very short, barely skimming her behind. In fact, if she bent over at all, it would definitely reveal a hell of a lot more than was decent.

Good God! She thought. *It's a bloody good thing we're not going out anywhere. There is no way I could wear this dress out in public.*

After putting on the heels she walked out of her dressing room into the bedroom, and again he was there waiting for her.

As she walked in he looked at her, giving her that stare that always sent tingles up and down her spine.

"Good." He said quietly. "You look amazing. That dress is perfect."

He didn't smile, just looked at her, then extending his hand, he finally spoke. Tonight he was in a mood she'd never seen before. It was a bit scary in fact, he was so serious. Still not smiling he grabbed her hand.

"Come. It's time for dinner."

Without a further glance at her, he led her down the stairs and onto the patio.

* * * *

He had hired the musicians again, but this time he'd

obviously asked them to play in the garden below and she had to admit she was glad. This dress was much too revealing.

The dinner was very good as always, and as they ate he asked her about her day, then told her about his.

He was very charming, very pleasant, but he said only what was necessary to keep the conversation going, and the whole time his eyes stared deeply into hers.

He didn't smile.

Not once.

He was very quiet, almost brooding, and through the whole meal she could feel the sexual tension building between them.

Once in a while, when he was handing her something, her fingers would brush against his and she could feel the tingles starting all over again.

They always had wine with their dinner, but tonight he urged her to have a glass of dessert wine as well. She was starting to feel very mellow, very relaxed and as he watched her finish her glass she saw him softly smile for the first time that evening, then getting up from his chair, he extended his hand to her once more.

"Come." He said, his eyes staring piercingly into hers.

"It's time."

Without saying another word he turned towards the French doors and led her towards the stairs.

. . .

The way he had looked at her all through dinner had been very unnerving, Alina thought.

He looked like a man on a mission and she had a horrible feeling she knew what it was.

Could she really do this?

She wasn't at all sure, wasn't at all confident she wanted to even try, but at this point she knew she no longer had a choice.

Standing by his bed, she felt him come up behind her and softly bending his head he kissed her neck.

"You looked incredibly sexy tonight." He said, "Incredibly sensual. I'm looking forward to finding out just how sensual you can be for me."

Unzipping her dress he pulled it off, leaving her with her stockings and shoes. Picking her up he lay her on the bed, then looking down at her, his eyes full of lust, he took of her shoes.

Quickly undressing, his eyes never leaving her face, he threw each piece of his clothing onto the floor to join her dress, then naked, he reached into the drawer and pulled out a condom, but this time after putting it on he reached into the drawer again and brought out a small vial of pills.

Still looking at her, he opened it and removing a couple, quickly swallowed them, then took a drink from the glass of water on the nightstand beside him.

. . .

What the hell? Alina thought, *What's he taking? Drugs?*

She didn't like the way this was going and he must have seen how she felt. As he lay down beside her, he stroked her face, still looking at her.

"Don't worry." He said quietly. "These won't make me high. They'll just help me last longer." Then kissing her ear he whispered,

"I want you to go as far as you can for me tonight, and I'm going to go with you."

As she felt those tingles starting yet again, he bent his head and kissed her breasts, his fingers playing with her nipples.

Just as he had that morning, he took his time, playing with her, making her want him more and more but never letting her come.

Once he could see she couldn't stand it much longer, he pushed into her, and once she started to come, he kissed her neck and quickly pulled out, then as soon as he saw she'd reached her peak, he'd thrust into her again, and again it would start, getting stronger and stronger each time.

It was one continuous never-ending orgasm, and after she'd come for him at least a dozen times, it was so strong that she started to shake again.

But he wouldn't allow it to end, ramming into her with more and more force, making her come over and over again.

. . .

She had long since lost track of how many times she'd come and time stopped having any meaning as the waves of pleasure kept rolling over her, getting stronger and stronger each time he made her come, until they started to get unbearable.

Her body was still shaking and every part of her felt like it was on fire. It was incredible pleasure and incredible pain all at the same time, and she didn't know how much more she could stand, but still her body wanted him.

Still it came for him each time he thrust into her, and instead of subsiding, the wanting was just getting stronger.

Each time he pushed into her, each time another orgasm would start, it was so strong she would scream out, but still he wouldn't stop.

Whenever she had breath enough to speak, she would beg him.

"Oh God. Oh God, Bear. Please. I can't take this." She would plead, and each time he would just keep looking at her.

"Yes. You can." He'd say, determined, his voice gruff with passion, then he would ram into her again, and again she would scream, but she no longer knew whether it was from pain or from pleasure.

The feelings she was experiencing each time he moved inside her now was like nothing she could have ever imagined.

It hurt so much, yet at the same time It felt so good, and even though it was all so intense she could hardly bear it, she never wanted him to stop.

It seemed to go on for hours.

As long as her body came for him he wouldn't let it stop. No matter how much she begged, he was determined to see how far it would go for him.

She was swimming in a sea of pain and pleasure now. She was screaming, crying, her whole body vibrating with his every touch, and still it wanted him.

Then finally, at long last, it started to subside.

Now, when he pushed into her, her body no longer reacted as strongly. It had finally reached its limit, and seeing that, he thrust into her hard several more times then she felt him come.

She lay there totally spent.

Unable to move.

Her face wet with tears. Even breathing seemed an effort.

After a few minutes, as her body slowly returned to normal and she started to breathe normally again, she slowly opened her eyes.

. . .

He was looking at her, his eyes soft with emotion.

"Fuck." He said quietly, wiping the tears from her face. "That was the most incredible thing I've ever experienced. I lost track of how many times you came for me before your body finally gave up. "

"Seeing how much you wanted me, how much your body was prepared to endure for me, how totally exhausted you were after giving me all you had .... That was bloody amazing Ally." He said quietly, still looking at her. Then he slowly smiled.

"You just kept coming and coming for what seemed like hours. Even with these pills I didn't know if I'd be able to last, but thankfully they worked."

" God, it was so worth it Love." He added softly. "I know I really pushed you to your limit, but your body still wanted me, was still willing to go there for me."

"And being inside you while you were constantly coming, your body vibrating, convulsing around me every time I touched you, it was amazing. I've never enjoyed anything so much in my life."

Softly stroking her hair he looked deep into her eyes.

"And now you know Love. Now we both know what your body is willing to do for me."

Drawing her to him, his arm around her, he kissed her neck, softly whispering.

. . .

"Get some sleep Love. After that, you'll need to recover, but by the morning you'll be ready again, and already I can hardly wait."

Fuck! Alina thought, totally exhausted still, *he wants me to do this again in the morning?*

What the hell have I started here!

FOURTEEN

The next morning, she woke again to the feel of his kisses on her neck.

Oh God! She thought, *I just can't do this again.*

Just as she was thinking this, he turned her towards him and looking deeply into her eyes, he smiled softly at her.

"You're doing it again Ally. Your trying to resist me again. Don't you know by now you can't?"

He kissed her, and she felt herself melting again in his arms.

He was right, she thought, *I can't resist him.*

I have no clue where this is all going to take me, how I'm ever going to be able to stand doing this every day while I'm here with him, but if that's what it takes to please him, then that's what I will do.

I'm too hooked on this man now to fight him any longer.

. . .

He was looking at her seriously now.

"What you did for me last night .... That was amazing Ally." He said quietly, stroking her face, but I don't expect you to do that every day. It was amazing, and now I know what your body will do for me."

Hearing his words, she sighed with relief, but it was short lived.

"In a couple of days, we'll try it again. With constant practice your body will be willing to do more. Now that I've experienced it, I want it again, but when you push your body to the limit like that you need to take time to recover."

"I think that's a good compromise." he continued, oblivious to her look of horror.

"It won't wear you out, and in between the practice will help your body give me even more next time."

"I've got some stronger pills. With those I'll be able to last for at least an hour and maybe a bit more. When we get to the point where they stop working we'll know it's enough. No point in overdoing it."

Fucking hell! She thought, *an hour?*
   Is he totally crazy?

Seeing the expression on her face he softly smiled.

"Why do you constantly doubt me?

Don't you know by now I know what I'm talking about?

Your body wants me now Ally. It wants to give me as much as it can. You're finding that out for yourself.

Every time we stop now at ten or twelve your body wants more, doesn't it?" He asked her quietly, looking at her knowingly.

"Yes," she sighed. "It does." Still smiling he stroked her face,

"And I want to experience everything it has to give me.

You need to rest in between so you'll have to be content with a dozen or so, just to keep you in practice, but in a couple of days I'll take the pills and we'll try it again. See just how much longer we can go."

He looked deep into her eyes.

"You give me so much pleasure Ally," he whispered softly. "And I know it's just going to get better and better. I love that your body wants me so much. I can hardly wait to find out just how much further it's willing to go for me." He said softly, smiling.

"But for now, we'll take it easy. Just let your body decide what it wants to give me. Now the only question will be just how long I can last."

As he started to kiss her again, Alina remembered how much she'd wanted him. Even though it had been almost unbearable at times, her body had still wanted him.

. . .

Thinking about doing that again was incredibly scary.

He didn't just want a repeat, he wanted more.

He was determined to get as much as he could out of her, and it terrified her, but at the same time she knew that regardless of how much pain there was along with the pleasure, she would do it for him.

It was true.

Her body craved him now, and whatever he wanted her to do for him she would do it.

Laying back on his pillow, Bear smiled.

"I told you Love you'd surprise yourself. Hell, you keep surprising me. Fourteen today before I finally couldn't take it any longer. That's not bad." He said, still smiling. Then he turned to look at her.

"And you still wanted more, didn't you." He said. It wasn't a question. They both knew it was a fact.

"Yes," she said, sighing. "I still wanted more."

"Good." He said, softly kissing her, "I love that you want me so much, but having to restrain itself will do your body good. It will give it a chance to rest and once you let it go for its limit again, it will be ready to give me so much more. Thinking about that will keep me going until then."

Then his mood changed, and he started to laugh.

"Now let's get out of bed before Melinda comes pounding on the door again. Maybe we can be waiting for her for a change. I'm sure that will shock the hell out of her."

Smiling at her again, he kissed her one last time, then headed for his bathroom.

* * * *

That morning, sitting in the library once more, Alina thought about the evening before.

She still couldn't quite believe she'd managed to do it, but she had.

He was right.

Her body wanted him, and it was willing to do way more than she'd ever thought possible to please him.

She'd thought she was totally spent, totally worn out, yet this morning her body had wanted him again and had come for him over and over until he'd been the one who'd finally had to stop.

And now he wanted more.

He was just as hooked on it as she was, but he was the one who had all the power, and what he wanted he would get.

It's bloody scary, she thought, *how hooked on him I am. How much my body wants him.*

The more he pushed her the more willingly she did what he asked.

Just like him, she now was just as eager to know how far her body could go.

. . .

But what would happen when he pushed her too far?

That was too scary to even think about.

He was like an addiction now. He was bringing out a side of her she hadn't known existed and this was incredibly exciting but also incredibly foolish, and yes, incredibly dangerous.

This man is so fucking dangerous she thought.

He has money, power, he's incredibly handsome, and he knows exactly how to use all of that to get what he wants. When he wants a woman, once he sets his mind on her, decided he was going to have her, no woman could resist him. And he knew it.

He could afford to surround her in a net of temptation, lull her into submission, then hook her with his incredible love making, his irresistible charm, his confident, smooth ways, until she would do anything he wanted.

Once he wanted her, no woman, however strong could resist him. He was so fucking dangerous, and now, even though she hadn't believed it could possibly ever happen, he'd hooked her as well.

She needed to concentrate on her work and get it finished. If there was to be any possibility of her getting out of here unscathed, she needed to leave, and she had to do it very soon.

Bear had broken his usual routine and sat with her for an hour already, answering all the rest of her questions as he'd promised. She had more than enough now to finish.

She needed to get this done as soon as possible.

. . .

Tempting as he and the world he was opening up for her where, she needed to be sensible.

To be realistic.

This was just a game for him.

However much he was enjoying it right now, however much he still wanted her, it couldn't possibly last.

She was just one of his many conquests and he would discard her just as easily as he had all the rest. This man was never happy with one woman for long. Sooner or later he would tire of her and want to move on.

The problem was she was starting to love it too much here, starting to wish she could stay, but this wasn't her life, and she knew if she was honest with herself she really didn't want it to be.

The possibilities he'd shown her had tempted her, intrigued her, made her eager to follow him wherever he led her, and in doing this she'd turned into something she'd never thought would be possible.

She was now a plaything for this man.

For him this was just a temporary amusement, but for her this whole experience had been completely life-changing, totally mind-blowing.

He'd opened up her eyes to a whole new world of possibilities, and because she'd always loved to experience new places, new people, new things, he'd completely hooked her.

But this, this obsession of his to push her not just over her limit but to see how much over it he could push her, this was taking it too far.

It was exciting, tempting, and fucking bloody dangerous.

He was pushing her to take her body to places she hadn't known it could go, and the temptation of finding out if she could actually do it was making it impossible for her to resist him.

She was afraid of how this was all going to end, was sure continuing this would be the worst mistake of her life, but at this point she no longer had a choice.

There was something inside her pushing her, needing to find out just as much as he did, needing to know, and until she did she knew she would continue, regardless of the consequences.

When it was finally over she was sure the price she would end up paying for this knowledge would be very high.

Probably higher than she wanted to pay.

He'd turned her into somebody she no longer recognized, a woman she didn't want to be, doing things she'd never thought she would ever do.

She would never be able to forget how much he'd controlled her, how eager she'd been to do what he wanted.

Regardless of how much she might want to, she knew forgetting would never be an option.

. . .

But hopefully, once she finally left, was finally away from this man and the incredible power he had over her, she'd be able to successfully lock all of this away deep in her memory banks, throw away the key, and never think of it again.

FIFTEEN

By lunchtime she'd finished the article, had proofread it and was feeling very good about it. She was sure Gerald would love it.

If only Bear would agree.

That second part she'd written about him was good. Really good.

It would show the world a side of him that nobody had ever known existed, as well as make them realize that owning an island that was already a home to many came with responsibilities.

She was sure when people dreamt about having that kind of luxury that thought never crossed their mind, and it was time that it did.

She was not only highlighting him, she was also exposing a problem that most never thought about and maybe it could just help someone somewhere make a better decision.

Yes, it was an idealistic goal, but it was also possible.

Good writing made people think and that was what she'd always wanted to do with her articles. Make people think.

As she was finishing up, he walked into the room and smiled at her.

"How's it going?" he asked. "Getting everything done?"

"Yes. I'm finished Bear. Do you have a couple of minutes? I want to go over something with you."

"Sure," he said, still smiling and sitting down in his usual chair. "Shoot."

Taking a deep breath, she began.

"I've gotten to know a lot about you and your life while I've been here. A lot of things that aren't common knowledge. You've got a pretty bad image you know." She said, smiling.

"Everybody just sees you as a playboy. Which of course you are," she added, still smiling, "But I know now there is much more to you than that, and I think others should know that as well."

Alina took another deep breath. She had no idea what his reaction was going to be. After seeing how private he had been about his family, he might feel that way about this as well.

Who knew? But the only way she'd find out was to give him the article and see.

"You hired me to write this article for you, but we're also

your PR firm. We have a responsibility to help you create a good image. I think this article I've written will go a long way to doing that."

He was looking at her cautiously now and she knew she was probably walking on shaky ground, but she pressed on.

"I've written two versions of the second part Bear. The first one is what I originally planned. It's okay. It will definitely do the job, but the second version is about the island."

"You showed me a thoughtful caring side that no one has ever really seen, and I've tried to highlight that. I think also making people aware that owning an island comes with responsibilities, that it's not just a luxury to be taken for granted, is a good thing as well."

Seeing he was still looking at her cautiously, she reached for the folder she'd prepared for him and handed it to him.

"Here. I've printed copies for you. You have last say of course. It's up to you which version you choose to print, and of course we will go along with whatever you decide." Then she looked at him, serious now.

"But please consider going with my second version Bear. Really consider it. I think it will be a good thing for both you and for the island."

Then she sat back, waiting for his reaction. He just looked at her for a minute, then he smiled.

"Okay. I'll take this with me and read it now while I wait for my conference call. I'll let you know later what I decide."

Then his gaze softened, and as he got up he walked up to her, kissing her on the head.

"Now that you're finished, why don't you go out and get some sun? Enjoy yourself for a bit.

The plane won't be back for another three days. Might as well have a bit of a break before you have to go back to work."

Still looking at her, he kissed her head again, and sighing, walked out of the room.

I wonder what that sigh was about? Alina thought as she watched him walk out.

Then her mind went back to her article. It was damn good, and it painted him in a very good light. Hopefully he'd see that as well. She'd done all she could. Now it was up to him.

* * * *

That evening she found another dress on the bed. This time it was a simple cotton sundress with a bag of beautiful white silk underwear and some white sandals.

He definitely has varied tastes. She thought with a smile, but she was enjoying dressing up for him so why not?

He was wearing a casual striped shirt and casual beige pants when she walked out of her dressing room and into the bedroom, and he smiled when he saw her.

"You look amazing Ally, as always Love." He said.

"I thought we'd have a casual dinner for a change. Melinda's cooking up some wings and ribs for us." Then still smiling he took her hand and walked towards the door.

As they walked out to the terrace, she saw the group was playing there again, and this time they were playing jazz. It was cheerful and upbeat, and he laughed and joked with her while they ate.

The wings and ribs were messy, certainly not the kind of meals she'd enjoyed with him so far, yet he seemed to enjoy them just as much if not more.

He had a couple of beers with his dinner, and as she looked at him tapping his feet to the music, she marveled yet again at the many facets of this man's personality.

When they were having their coffee, he got serious.

"I read the article, Alina, both versions." He said quietly.

Alina held her breath.

Would he let her print it?

As she looked at him, she could see he still looked serious. Was this a good sign or a bad one?

He was silent for a long time, then he sighed and looked at her.

"I usually don't talk about my private life." He said quietly. "People like to think the playboy image is the real me and I've always been happy to go along with that.

But what you wrote is really good, and it really made me think." He was still looking at her seriously as he continued.

. . .

"I had to think about it for a long time. Letting the world know about the island and my work here .... That's a big step, but I think you're right.

I think it's time I changed my image. Somehow, I just don't think it's going to suit me much longer."

He was looking searchingly into her eyes now, then after a minute he looked away, then looking back he smiled.

"Go ahead and print it. I think it's time." he said.

"I'm glad. So do I." Alina agreed, smiling back at him.

* * * *

That night after they'd made love again, he turned to her, and smiled.

"Sixteen? You're determined to push me to my limit, aren't you." he laughed. Then he stroked her face and sighed.

"I'm going to miss you when you leave, and that doesn't happen often Alina, believe me." He said, serious now.

"I don't really want to let you go. Yes, I've enjoyed a lot of women, I can't deny that, but nobody has made me as happy as you do." He said quietly.

"I think we'll have to keep seeing each other. I'll be in New York in a couple of weeks. Will you go out with me? It will create a lot of talk. You've got to be prepared for that, but I want to see where this goes."

He stroked her face again.

. . .

"Are you willing to do that love?" he asked her.

"I'm not a good bet. Never have been." He added with a sigh, "but with you, I want to try. What do you say?" he said, smiling at her now. "Are you up for it?"

Alina smiled back at him.

"Yes, Bear." She said softly, "I'm up for it. I want to try as well."

"Good." He replied, then cupping her body and drawing the covers over them both, he added,

"Now sleep love. Tomorrow morning we'll celebrate. You know how I love celebrating with you"

He softly kissed her neck, then with a happy sigh, he tightened his arms around her.

Snuggling up to him, Alina sighed as well.

What the hell had she done?

Was she crazy?

Hadn't she just told herself that she had to leave? Needed to get him out of her life as soon as she could?

Yet now she was agreeing to keep seeing him. Agreeing to try to make their relationship work.

And all because he'd said that was what he wanted.

That had been all it had taken, and the thought of how easily she'd agreed terrified her.

Obviously, regardless of how sensibly she'd made herself

look at it, underneath all the logical reasoning, she'd still wanted to keep him in her life.

This man pushed her buttons like nobody had ever done before. The things her body was willing to do for him .... It was unbelievable, and incredibly scary.

He demanded everything from her, was determined to push her to her limits, and she would willingly go there for him.

He had hooked her, hook, line and sinker, and now there was no escape.

Obviously, whatever it took to keep him in her life, she would do it, whether it was the smart thing to do or not.

She knew that now, however unwise this was, however much it terrified her, she wanted this.

He was tempting her with words that even though she hadn't consciously known it, she'd obviously been waiting to hear, and even though the sensible logical part of her still very much questioned the wisdom of it whole thing, deep inside, regardless of how utterly crazy it was, how utterly unlikely that it could work, she wanted this to work, just as much as he said he did.

Who knew where this was going to go?

He wasn't a man who did relationships. As he said, he wasn't a good bet and he certainly wasn't making any promises, but he'd told her he was willing to try.

She had a feeling that was much more than he'd offered

any other woman before, and as far as she was concerned, just hearing him speak those words to her had been enough.

She was still hooked on him, would always be hooked on him, and until he decided he wanted to walk away, she wasn't strong enough to leave him.

There was no point in even trying to fight this any longer.

This was her fate.

SIXTEEN

The next day Alina emailed Gerald the finished article, and a couple of hours later he answered her.

"Amazing! Brilliant work Alina. Much better than I ever could have expected. It will go out next week. Hurry back. We need to talk about your future."

Alina smiled happily as she read the email.

She had done it.

She'd impressed Gerald and she was now pretty sure that promotion was hers. But surprisingly, she found that didn't make her as happy as she'd thought it would.

Yes, she was glad that the article had gone over well. She'd always wanted to be a writer, had always love to write, and couldn't see ever stopping, but somehow now, it didn't seem like enough.

. . .

Determined not to think about why that was, Alina closed her laptop.

The plane was due to arrive the next day. She would be going back to work, to her life in New York, and that was what she had to concentrate on.

Bear had said he wanted to keep seeing her there, and she was glad of that, but really, was that ever going to lead anywhere?

He was happy with her now, he was anxious to see how much more she could push herself for him, and as long as she kept giving him more and more of what he wanted, he would be content, but a man like him was never content for long.

She could only push herself so far, and once she'd reached her limit he would move on to someone else.

That's what he'd always done.

There was no reason to think he wasn't going to do that with her as well.

But she'd enjoy it while she could, Alina thought with a sigh.

It had been three days now since he'd pushed her limits the first time, and tonight he was planning on doing it again.

The thought was bloody scary, but she was also looking forward to it.

Looking forward to finding out just how much she could push herself for him.

* * * *

It had turned colder now.

Bear had told her that there was a storm North of them, and that was why they were getting this weather, but after the hot days they'd had all the time she'd been there, neither one of them would be comfortable on the patio, so they ate inside instead.

He had a table set up for them in his suite, and as she ate her meal with him she was thankful that Melinda had made up the fire.

A week ago she hadn't believed they ever had any need to use the fireplace, but she could see now that she'd been wrong.

It had been a cold, dull day and the blazing fire was warm and cheery. As she looked at it she smiled and turned to him.

"So, are we making love on the fur rug tonight?" she asked him, smiling. She was sure that was why he had it, but again he surprised her.

Looking at her, he laughed.

"I don't blame you for assuming that." He said, "It is after all what people would expect of me, but believe it or not, I prefer a comfortable bed. I guess I'm old fashioned that way." He smiled looking deep into her eyes.

"Besides, I have much more in mind for us tonight than a quick lay in front of the fire."

Alina sighed. That was what she was afraid off.

An hour?

She was pretty sure there was no way that was going to happen, regardless of what he said.

* * * *

As she walked up to the bed, he was right behind her, and when she stopped he bent and kissed her neck.

"I've been thinking about this so long Love." He said, "I want you so much it hurts."

Taking off her clothes he lay her on the bed and then took of his own. As he got out a condom and a vial of pills, she found herself trembling.

Could she really do this again?

She knew now that along with the pleasure, there would also be pain, but she also knew she was willing to do it for him.

If this was what would make him happy then regardless of how painful it was, she would do it.

As before he took his time, playing with her until she could no longer take it.

"Oh God, Bear." She moaned. "I need you inside me."

She heard him catch his breath, then he thrust into her and she started to come.

As always, the first few were very mild, but gradually they became longer and harder to take. Again, she lost count as one orgasm melted into the other, and all she could experience was the pleasure that was constant now as he kept thrusting into her.

But slowly, like before, they got harder and harder to take, and soon she was screaming each time she started to come. Along with the pleasure there was pain now, and it was almost unbearable, but it gradually turned to pleasure as she'd known it would.

She had no idea how long she'd been coming.

She'd lost all track of time.

All she could do was feel.

The pain was increasing and so was the pleasure and it was becoming almost impossible to take, but still her body wanted him, came for him, and still he made her come.

He was ramming into her hard now, and even though the pain was excruciating when she started coming, it quickly turned into exquisite pleasure.

She'd never felt anything like this before and she found as each one diminished she was anxious for the next one to start, even though she knew the pain would come first.

It seemed to her she'd been coming for hours.

There had been no end to it, and even though the pain made her scream, she no longer bothered to beg him to stop. She knew it was useless. Regardless of how much she screamed he was going to make her ride it out until the end.

Then after what seemed like an eternity, the pain gradually started to take over.

It lasted longer, and there was less and less of the pleasure, but her body still wanted him.

She was crying now, sobbing uncontrollably, and each time she started to come she screamed in agony.

As she was thinking it was all too much to bear, that she would surely die of this, she felt him thrust into her several times more, then finally come.

As the final orgasm finally dissipated and her body slowly started to recover, he took her in his arms, wiping her tears, and stroking her face, as she still sobbed.

It took her several minutes to finally catch her breath, and as she opened her eyes she saw he was looking at her, his eyes filled with concern.

She said the first thing that came into her mind.

"I was still coming, but you stopped. You've never done that before."

He was still looking at her, and as he saw she had stopped shaking, he softly kissed her."

"You gave me almost an hour Love. That was enough."

His eyes still filled with concern, he slowly stroked her hair.

"I could see all you were feeling was pain. That was never my goal Ally.

I want to see you enjoy yourself. Giving you pain is the last thing I want to do. It was enough." His eyes were glistening now as he looked at her.

. . .

Are those tears? She thought, amazed. *He's crying?*

"I'm sorry love." He said to her quietly, his eyes still on her face.

"We're never going to push it this far again. I can't stand to see you suffer. I love you Ally. I'm never going to cause you any more pain."

He drew her in his arms, and kissing her head, he gently drew the sheets around them.

"Now sleep Love. "He said, softly, as his arms tightened around her.

Totally exhausted still, she closed her eyes and slept.

* * * *

The next morning, she woke up to his kisses again.
Oh God! She thought, *I can't do this anymore!*

But he didn't turn her towards him the way he usually did, he just kept kissing her and holding her, drawing her body next to his, and even though she could feel he was aroused again, he just kept kissing her, and stroking her hair.

Finally, she turned to him and she could see he still looked concerned.

"How are you feeling Love?" he asked her softly, and the look of concern in his eyes tugged at her heart.

This man really cares, she thought. *He really cares for*

me, and as she smiled at him, she could feel her heart opening up to him.

"I feel much better. Fine in fact." She said, still smiling. "So, what happened to my morning fuck?"

He grinned at her then, and as he moved over her, she tightened her arms around him.

God! she wanted this man, she thought, as he thrust into her.

She came again, but this time he didn't prolong it. After a few minutes she felt him thrust into her several times in a row, then come himself.

As he fell back onto his pillow, his eyes closed, she was still catching her breath as she turned and looked at him.

She would always want him. she thought. *It was inevitable now, and yes, she loved him as well.*

He'd said he loved her last night.

Maybe it had just been an emotional response. Probably he didn't mean it, but she knew she did.

She loved this man with all her heart, and deep inside her she knew that would never change.

SEVENTEEN

As he opened his eyes, he turned and took her in his arms again. He didn't say anything, just looked at her, but his eyes were filled with emotion.

After a moment he kissed her, then softly stroked her hair.

"I meant what I said last night Ally." He said quietly. "I love you. I don't know how it happened, and it's certainly never happened to me before, but I definitely love you."

"I love you too Bear." She said softly, and as he looked into her eyes she knew he could see it was true.

As they were still lying there, just looking at each other, their arms around each other, there was a sudden pounding on the door.

"Mr. Bear. Mr. Bear." They heard Melinda call, and she

sounded worried. "Mr. Bear. Emanuel is here. He needs to talk to you and it's important."

Gone was her usual playful manner.

She sounded worried and afraid, and as Alina looked up at the door, she saw Bear quickly get out of bed.

"Be right there Melinda." He called out, "Tell him to wait in my office. I'll just put on some pants."

Before she had a chance to reply, he'd already disappeared into his bathroom.

Two minutes later he was back wearing his jeans and pulling on a T-shirt while he walked hurriedly to the door.

Remembering he had company, he walked over to the bed and gave her a quick kiss.

"Emanuel never comes here unless it's really important. I've got to go Love. See you later."

Then he disappeared out to the hall.

Alina had just dressed when she heard Melinda knock on the door again, and she opened it to see her standing there, her face looking strained.

"Too cold for the patio this morning Missy." She said, "I've put your breakfast tray in Bear's living room across the hall."

Melinda was usually bright and cheerful. This was very unusual for her.

. . .

"What's going on Melinda?" she asked her. "Is something wrong?"

"There's a storm coming Missy." She said, "A big one. Storms are bad news here."

Her face held a worried frown as she hurried away.

Alina went into the living room and sat down on the couch by the coffee table where Melinda had deposited her tray and poured herself a cup of the coffee.

A storm? Bear had said there was one North of them, but she knew storms could easily switch course. And very quickly.

The plane was supposed to be there in a few hours. The best thing she could do was stay here and pack her things. If they were busy getting ready for the storm she'd just get in the way.

As she was finishing her toast and coffee, Bear walked into the room and sat down on the couch beside her. He looked worried.

"Sorry Love." He said, "You're not going to be going anywhere today. The plane won't be coming.

With these high winds it's not safe. I have to go help Emanuel get things locked up. It's likely to take a few hours. The storm is supposed to hit this afternoon."

He looked at her with concern. "Will you be okay here by yourself?"

"Of course." She answered, "But is there anything I can do to help?"

"No Love, not really." He replied. "It's all heavy manual work. Emanuel will need help. I've rounded up some of the other men as well."

As she put her hand on his arm, she looked at him, her eyes full of concern.

"Be careful Bear." She said. "Please be careful. I don't want anything to happen to you."

He smiled then and leaned down and kissed her.

"You're worried about me? Don't be Love." He said, "We've been through these storms before. We have an emergency procedure all worked out and everyone knows the drill."

Then he grinned at her wickedly.

"But it's nice to see you're worried about me. You can show me how glad you are I'm back safely tonight. I'll look forward to it."

With one last parting kiss he got up and hurried back out the door.

Well, I guess there's no point in packing, Alina thought to herself.

She was glad she was going to get to spend more time with him, but she would have preferred if it had happened under a lot more pleasant circumstances.

* * * *

It was almost lunchtime when he returned. He looked tired and worried and this made Alina worried as well.

Nothing usually got to Bear. He took most things in his

stride. Just as Melinda had said, storms were obviously a big deal here.

As he walked into the living room where she'd been trying not very successfully to read, she could see his jeans and top where smeared with oil and covered with dirt. Coming over to her, he gave her a kiss.

"Well, I think we're ready." He said sighing, "Or at least as ready as we can be. With storms you just never know where they'll hit or how bad they will be. We'll just have to keep our fingers crossed that this one isn't too bad and doesn't last long."

Then he smiled down at her.

"I'm filthy. I'm going to shower and put on some clean clothes. Melinda will bring us in a lunch tray soon. Must say I'm starving."

With a last smile he disappeared out the door once more.

When he appeared ten minutes later he looked more relaxed.

Obviously, the shower had done him good. As he walked in Melinda followed with a large tray, and he turned, taking it from her.

"Thanks Melinda. I'll take it from here. Everything okay in the house?"

"Yes Mr. Bear, everything's fine." She replied.

"The men you sent over put on the shutters. We should be ready."

Alina looked over then to the French doors and noticed that metal shutters had been pulled over them as well.

Seeing all these preparations was starting to make her scared.

Were storms really such a big thing here?

Everyone certainly seemed to be very worried. Hopefully like Bear said this one wouldn't last long.

Melinda had made them beef stew for lunch and Bear ate heartily. As she watched him Alina realized that he had run out this morning without any breakfast. He hadn't even had any coffee. Then he'd spent hours doing manual labor. Little wonder he was starving.

She marveled yet again at how involved he got with what went on here.

A lot of land owners in his position would expect their staff to take care of everything, but he was right out there with the rest of them helping them to get ready.

Another admirable trait she thought with a smile. His point book was certainly filling up.

After they finished eating, instead of working in his office the way he usually did, Bear went and got his laptop, then set it up on the dining table and worked quietly while she read.

Melinda had set the fire for them again and the flames were warm and comforting.

Outside she could hear the wind getting stronger and stronger and every once in a while, she would hear branches hitting the shutters. Once she even heard a crash. As she looked at Bear questioningly, he looked back at her, his face serious.

"That sounds like a tree down to me." He said quietly. "Not good."

Still looking serious, he gave the shuttered doors one last glance then returned with determination to his work.

They spent the rest of the day together and in the evening, Melinda brought them another tray with their dinner.

There were no musicians and fancy evening clothes now, but she could see everyone was too worried to care about such things. What was happening around them was the only thing anyone could think about.

When they went to bed that night, he made love to her with an increased passion she hadn't seen before. She came for him eight times, and the last time he came as well.

"That's enough." He said resolutely, as he lay back, his arm around her.

"I love seeing you come for me Ally, but I want to see you're enjoying it as well. I've been pushing you too hard and that's not going to happen again." he said grinning,

"I know it's hard for you to control yourself now when it comes to me, but I want to make sure I keep you keen."

Still grinning, he kissed her once more, and drawing the covers around them, settled them both down to sleep.

EIGHTEEN

The wind was still howling when she woke, and as she lay there listening to it, she felt him put his arms around her and kiss her neck.

"Morning love." He whispered, then turning her to face him she saw he was grinning.

"As you put it so succinctly yesterday, are you ready for your morning fuck?"

She laughed as she answered him, putting her arms around him.

"Always." She whispered, and he looked back at her, still grinning.

"That's one of your most lovable traits Ally." He said, grinning wickedly at her now. "The way you love being fucked by me, and I'm more than happy to oblige." He added, his eyes hungry now as he moved over her.

"Always."

* * * *

As they sat in the living room having their breakfast, Melinda came in, her face white and worried.

"Oh Mr. Bear." She said, and they could see she was close to tears. Bear immediately got up, putting his arm around her, his face filled with concern.

"What's wrong Melinda?" he asked

"It's Pedro. He's missing," Melinda replied, her eyes filled with fear.

"He went out to get that dog when Jimena wasn't looking, and he never came back. She's in the kitchen now, crying. Emanuel's with her. He's going to go out to look for him, but he didn't want to leave her alone."

Then still looking immensely worried, she looked up at him.

"The roads are terrible now. Emanuel had a hell of a time getting them here. He wants to know if you can round up some of the men to help."

Bear didn't wait to reply. He just hurried out the door.

Alina got up and put her arm around the now sobbing woman.

"It will be all right Melinda. They'll find him." and as she comforted her she prayed with all her heart they would.

A little boy, out alone in this storm? How could he survive it?

Melinda finally calmed down and Alina followed her down to the kitchen where Jimena sat huddled at the table. Her tear-streaked face full of fear. As they walked in, she looked at them.

"Oh Melinda." She sobbed. "He's just a little boy. He'll never survive out there."

Hearing his wife, Emanual immediately walked over to her and put his arms around her, kissing her head.

"We'll find him Jima." He said, his voice filled with determination. "With Bear's help we'll find him."

Kissing her once more he walked over to join Bear.

Bear was busy on his cell phone, texting, and within a few minutes a group of men had gathered in the kitchen. He'd spread a map on the kitchen table and was systematically dividing the area around their home in sections and assigning one to each man.

As she listened to him quietly and calmly talking to them, she marveled yet again at how much he cared for these people.

They were family for him now she realized, and he was willing to do almost anything for them.

Soon they were heading out the door, and as he put on his jacket, Bear came over and kissed her head.

"Take care of Jimena Love." He said, "We'll find him, and let's pray to God he's okay." He added quietly, not wanting the rest of them to hear.

Alina, put her hand on his arm.

"Be careful Bear. Please be careful." She said, her voice filled with concern. "I love you." She added softly.

He looked down on her then and softly smiled.

"I love you." He said quietly, then he turned and hurried out the door.

* * * *

As the women waited together in the kitchen, the storm continued to rage outside. Every once in a while, one of the men would return and report back. Nobody had found any trace of Pedro yet, but the storm seemed to be dying down slightly.

It was still bad, but it wasn't as bad as some of the other ones had been, one of the men had told her, though his eyes still looked worried.

"At least it isn't getting any worse." Alina told herself. "He'll be alright. He has to be. He'll be alright."

They searched unsuccessfully all day. Pedro wasn't at any of the usual places Emanuel had told them he frequented, and she could see when they huddled together in the corner warming up with the hot coffee Melinda had made them, that they were starting to get worried.

She was as well.

All the men had returned now, even Emanuel, but Bear still wasn't back.

As the sun set and night descended upon them, she started to really get afraid.

Where could he be?

It was so bad out there.

All kinds of things could have happened to him, and as she started to think that thought she blocked it from her mind with determination.

This isn't helping, she told herself firmly. *You're not helping by getting upset. These people are upset enough. They don't need to worry about you as well.*

She got up and walked over to where Melinda was peeling potatoes.

"Here, I'll do that." She said to her quietly, putting her arm around her. Melinda looked up at her thankfully.

"That will be a big help. I'll start on the stew. Everyone is going to be hungry when they get back."

Determined to stop worrying, Alina put her mind on her task.

Melinda was right. They would need food, and at least this was one way she could help.

NINETEEN

Melinda made Emanuel and Jimena stay in one of the guest bedrooms that night. When Emanuel protested, saying he would drive them back home she looked at him angrily.

"And what help will it be if you go out and get yourself killed on those bloody roads? Bear told me to get a room ready for you before he left and that's where you're going to stay."

Not allowing him to argue with her any longer, she turned with determination to the stew that was now simmering on the stove.

The next morning Alina sat in the kitchen sipping coffee. Her fingers were shaking as she lifted the cup to her lips.

Bear hadn't returned.

She'd sat up long into the night waiting for him, finally falling asleep on the living room couch, still in her clothes, wanting to see him as soon as he was back, but he'd never returned.

. . .

The storm was still raging.

The sun had just risen, and she was the first one up, the rest of the searchers still in their beds getting a well-deserved sleep.

But she couldn't sleep.

Until he was back she knew she wouldn't be able to sleep and going to bed would be a total waste of time.

As she sat there trying to calm herself down, she made herself look at this logically. Made herself think.

Emanuel and the rest of the men were going to extend their search today. There wasn't anyone to go looking for Bear. They all had much more important things to do.

It was up to her.

She looked at the map still spread out on the table.

Bear had written each man's name down in the section he'd been assigned to search. She could see where Bear had gone, and she knew it wasn't that far from the house.

The storm was still raging outside and the roads, from what all the men who had returned reported, were totally unnavi-gable now, covered with mud, but this particular section of jungle was within walking distance.

The other day he'd told her about a trail that led through that area and pointed out where the entrance was. He'd told her it was a great trail for hiking.

Probably not so great today, she thought to herself, worriedly, *but at least there's a trail.*

Something must have happened to him.

He wouldn't have stayed out all night if he could have made it back. Something must have happened.

I'm going to find him, she thought to herself, even more determined now. *I'm going to find that bloody man if it's the last thing I do.*

Once she'd made up her mind and decided what she was going to do, Alina had prepared with care.

She wasn't stupid.

She knew that if she was going to survive out there in that storm she would need supplies, and when she found him after being out all night he would need food and especially water.

She packed a few bottles of water and a first aid kit into a small backpack she found in the corner of the pantry and added a bag of walnut halves and a few chocolate bars from one of the shelves.

There wasn't much more in the way of food she could carry but these would do. Hadn't she read chocolate would give you energy in these kinds of situations?

She put it on over her jacket, thankful that it wasn't very heavy. Grabbing a flashlight she'd found in the hall and hoping and praying she wouldn't need to use the first aid kit, she knew she was as ready as she could be, and taking a deep breath, she walked out of the house.

* * * *

As she made her way to where Bear had told her the trail started, she could feel the wind slashing at her face.

It was cold and wet, and she had to bow her head to continue, but she was determined. It wasn't so strong that she couldn't walk in it.

She could do this.

After a few minutes of hunting she found the opening leading into the jungle and started to make her way down the overgrown trail.

Now that she was in the jungle, thankfully the wind wasn't as strong, but she could still hear it howling around her as she walked.

As she made her way, shining her flashlight in front of her, she could see all the damage that had already been done. There were broken branches everywhere and every once in while she'd come upon a tree lying across the trail.

After an hour when she hadn't seen any sign of him she started to worry.

Could he really have gone this far? It was possible, she thought. *Anything was possible.*

It was daylight now, and even though the rain beat down on

her mercilessly and her rain jacket was no longer giving her much protection, the wind had subsided slightly.

One way or another she would find him.

There was no bloody way she was going to give up.

At least I don't have to worry about the light disappearing. Alina thought. *I'm going to keep looking until I find that man if it takes me all bloody day.*

TWENTY

After another half hour she heard a sound ahead of her on the trail.

It sounded like someone crying, and hoping and praying that she'd finally found him, she started to run.

As she rounded the next corner she saw him lying on the ground just ahead of her.

He was holding Pedro in his arms and trying to soothe him. Chico was standing next to them, wining. Pedro was the one she'd heard crying.

There was a huge tree lying across one of Bear's legs, and she realized he was trapped.

This is why he hadn't returned.

He couldn't move.

She ran up to him, crying now and putting her arms around

him, she covered his face with kisses.

"Oh Bear. I found you." She sobbed. "I found you."

He put his arm around her, but as she looked at him she could see he was in pain. He was also soaked to the skin, having taken off his jacket and put it around Pedro.

"What the hell are you doing here Ally?" he said to her, his voice weak. "You shouldn't be out here. It's dangerous."

She looked back at him then, calmer now.

"You think? How did this happen?"

"I was making my way back with Pedro and Chico when the tree fell.

It was my fault. I was an idiot. I knew in this weather I needed to be careful. I should have noticed what was happening, but Pedro was crying, and I was trying to soothe him and I wasn't looking where I was going."

"What happened to your cell?' she asked.

"It's over there." He sighed, indicating the phone that was lying several feet away from them.

"When I fell it flew out of my pocket. I heard it crack as it hit that rock. Pretty sure it's had the biscuit. It won't be of any use to anyone now."

Then he looked at her with determination.

"I can't move, and you can't help me Ally." He said

quietly. "You'll have to leave me. Take Pedro and Chico and go back to the house. At least then I'll know you're all safe. Leave me here. There's nothing else you can do."

He was trapped, exhausted, and soaked. He'd already survived out here all night, but in his condition, he wouldn't survive much longer.

She needed to get him out of here.

"Bloody hell there isn't!" she said to him, determined now. "I'm not leaving you here in this storm. There's no way. I'm going to get you out. One way or another I'll get you out."

He looked at her, angry now.

"Don't be crazy." He said to her sharply. "There's nothing you can do. Take Pedro and go."

"Just shut up and let me think." she said, as she saw him close his eyes in pain. There was no bloody way she was going to leave him.

As she looked at him Alina furiously racked her brain.

She'd heard of women moving cars to free someone they loved but she knew that was pretty much a long shot. There must be another way.

Think. She told herself, *think.*

Then she remembered a long-ago science class. Wasn't there something about levers she'd learned?

Something about moving heavy objects with the help of a lever?

She remembered a long-ago science experiment.

Unfortunately, at the time she'd been a lot more interested in her good-looking partner than in what she was doing.

Think Alina, think! She demanded of herself. *Some small particle of knowledge must have lodged itself into that sixteen-year-old boy-crazy brain.*

As she racked her brain, trying desperately to remember, it started to come back to her.

She needed a pivot and something flat to move the log. She also needed something to put under it to keep it lifted while she got his leg out from under it.

Looking around she saw the ground was littered with debris, obviously the result of the storm.

Normally not such a good thing, she thought, *but maybe today it will work in my favor.*

If there was any bloody way at all to make this work, she was going to find it.

He opened his eyes and looked at her and she could see he was weak. She took off her backpack and opening it, handed him some water.

He drank thankfully, then she handed the bottle to Pedro. Grabbing one of the chocolate bars, she quickly broke it into pieces.

"Here," she said, handing them both a large piece. "Eat this. You need to keep up your strength."

While Pedro munched happily on his piece, she broke a small piece for the dog who ate it greedily. She wasn't sure chocolate was good for dogs, but hell, it was all she had.

As she looked at them she noticed his leg was bleeding.

God only knows how bad it is under that bloody log, she thought, *but at least I can clean it up a bit.*

Taking out the first aid kit and opening it she noticed, thankfully, that it had been very well equipped. There were pain killers, antiseptic cream, and lots of bandages.

Good, she thought with a sigh, *a Band-aid certainly wouldn't cut it here.*

Leaning over his leg she cleaned the wound with a little of the water from the bottle, applied some of the cream, then bandaged his leg.

All the time she was working he looked at her.

When she applied the cream, she could see by his face that it hurt, but he didn't complain. When she'd finished and was congratulating herself on having done a half decent job, she looked up to see him smiling at her.

"You're a regular Florence Nightingale, aren't you?" he said, still smiling, but she could see he was in pain.

Reaching into the kit once again she picked up the bottle of pain killers. After reading the directions, she took out a couple and handed the to him with the bottle of water.

"Here, take these." She said, her face still full of concern. "They'll at least help a bit. Once I get you out of here you'll have to try and walk. Better save your strength."

"Your crazy Ally." He said with a sigh, "There's no way you can move that thing." But he swallowed the pills and drank down some more of the water.

"Watch me." She said to him with determination.

The rain was still beating down on them and the wind was howling. Every few minutes more branches would crash to the ground around them.

As she'd been bandaging his cut she'd seen a large tree come crashing down on the trail just in front of them.

The working conditions weren't ideal, that was for damn sure she thought, *but she'd have to cope.*

The rain was still beating down on them and now there was more and more chance of being felled by another falling tree on top of all that.

She needed to get him out of here and she needed to do it quickly.

She had no idea how the hell she was going to manage it,

but somehow, she was going to do this. There was no way she was leaving him here to die.

Now that she'd taken care of their immediate needs, she turned her mind back to the problem at hand.

Hunting around she quickly found what she needed. Positioning a log next to the one lying across his leg, she set up her lever.

The wood she was using wasn't ideal for this by any means, and the first few times she tried, it didn't move. But she was determined not to get discouraged.

Please God, let this work. She prayed, then she tried again, and finally she felt the log start to give.

It wasn't moving a lot, but it was moving.

It was a start.

She kept trying, kept working at it, and eventually she'd managed to lift it off the ground by almost a foot. Mustering all her strength, she moved it to the side and when she finally let it go she heard it crash on the log she'd laid beside it.

Somehow, she'd managed to move it enough so there was now a gap where his leg was, and it would be large enough for him to move his leg out from under.

"Bloody hell!" He said, looking up at her with admiration. "Where the hell did you learn to do that?"

"High school physics." She replied with a smile. "All in a day's work."

"Bloody hell!" he said again, but he was smiling.

It took her another half hour to slowly move his leg from under it. Thankfully, the way the tree had fallen, there was a large branch under the part that had fallen onto his leg, and by some miracle, that had protected him.

The tree had trapped his leg, but it hadn't actually been lying on it.

With a bit of luck, he'll still be able to walk on it, she thought, anxiously, and again she prayed.

When his leg was finally free, with her help, he managed to get up. Walking around, he looked up at her and smiled.

"I don't know how I got so bloody lucky, but there doesn't seem to be any damage." He said smiling. "Just the cut. Let's get out of here."

He walked slowly now, his leg stiff from spending so long under the tree, but at least he could walk.

As she looked at him, then kissed him on the cheek, he looked down on her and smiled. She could tell the medication, the water and the chocolate were making him feel much better already, and as he put his hand on her shoulder to steady himself, Alina gave a silent prayer of thanks.

It could have been so much worse, she thought. *So very much worse.*

TWENTY-ONE

They slowly made their way back, but it was slow going.

His leg was still stiff, and he was holding Pedro. Every ten minutes or so he had to stop.

It had taken Alina and hour and a half to find him and she knew at this rate it would probably take them twice as long to get back, but she didn't care. They were on their way back. That was all that mattered.

After an hour she could see he was tiring. There were some large rocks by the trail and she made him stop and sit down.

"We'll have a break." She said with determination. "I'll watch Pedro. You rest. But first I've got another chocolate bar and some walnuts. It will help you regain your strength."

He sat down smiling at her.

"You're getting very bossy you know that?" he said grinning. "I think tonight I'll have to remind you who's boss in this relationship."

The fact that he was up to joking and thinking about sex meant he was pretty much back to normal, and she grinned back at him.

" Really?" she said teasingly, "And how are you going to do that?"

"You'll find out tonight," he said, grinning at her wickedly, "and I can hardly wait." She smiled at him happily.

There was definitely nothing wrong with this man!

After they'd split the chocolate, and each had some walnuts and more water, they started off again.

He was holding up well, but after another fifteen minutes she saw him tire again. With determination she stopped by some more rocks.

"Time for a break." She said, "If you're going to be any good to me tonight, you'd better not use up all your strength."

"Oh, don't worry about that," he said grinning at her wickedly again. "Just thinking about what I'm going to do to you is giving me strength."

It was definitely affecting her as well. she thought. She could feel those tingles going up and down her spine each time he looked at her like that.

He wasn't the only one who could hardly wait, she thought smiling to herself.

· · ·

They'd been walking for just over an hour when they heard someone hurrying towards them, and after a minute Emanuel came into view.

"Daddy!" Pedro squealed in delight, running towards him, and as he knelt down and hugged his son, she saw there were tears in Emanuel's eyes.

"Oh, thank God!" He said, still hugging him. Then turning to Bear he asked. "Where did you find him."

"He'd gone up the trail looking for Chico." He replied, smiling as the dog barked and wagged its tail when it heard its name. Then he quickly explained what had happened.

"Thank God." Emanuel said again, then turning to Bear, he shook his hand. "Thanks." He said, and Bear grinned. "No problem."

The two men hugged, and Alina could see the love they both felt for each other.

He's built up some wonderful friendships here, she thought, watching them. And he really cares. *Little wonder the people here love him so much.*

Emanuel quickly pulled out his cell and called Jimena to tell her Pedro was safe, then he picked up Pedro in his arms. Looking at Bear, his face concerned, he asked.

"Are you okay to keep walking Bear? It's not too much further, but if you want I'll run back with Pedro then come back for you."

"I'm fine." Bear answered smiling, then he looked down at Alina lovingly. "Florence Nightingale here has taken good care of me."

Giving her a kiss, he leaned on her shoulder and pressed on with determination.

* * * *

That afternoon they sat in his living room again, the fire again blazing in front of them. She'd insisted he rest when he got back, and he'd smiled.

"You really are getting too bossy for your own good," he said grinning, "You really are asking for it, you know that?"

"Yep," she'd replied, grinning back at him. "I do."

He'd smiled wickedly at her then, but he hadn't fought her. Getting his laptop, he'd settled at the table again, working there quietly while she worked on her laptop as well.

The storm was still raging outside, but it seemed the worst was over now.

The major front had passed, and the weather was supposed to finally improve the next day. There had been a lot of damage Emanuel had told them, and there would be a lot of work to do, but not now.

Now they were just all thankful that everyone was safe, and it was time to rest and gather their strength.

Tomorrow would be soon enough.

They had an early supper that night.

Everyone was exhausted, and Bear didn't want anyone to be working late. Emanuel and Jimena had gone home with Pedro, and after she'd brought in their dinner tray he insisted Melinda take the rest of the evening off.

"You can get the tray tomorrow." He'd told her, smiling. "Just relax tonight. Watch one of those soaps you're so fond off."

She'd smiled at that, but she hadn't objected. They were all tired.

It had been a long day.

As he walked up to the bed with her, Bear put his arms around her and kissed her, then looked at her with that wicked look of his, but behind it she could also see the hunger that was slowly building.

"I think it's time you learned you're place Woman." He said quietly.

"You don't get to boss me around and get away with it. Your place is under me with your legs open wide, submitting to my every wish."

Then taking off her clothes, he lay her down on the bed. Soon he was lying next to her, his eyes filled with desire.

"Let's see how good you are at following my orders for a change." He murmured, as he leaned over her, his hand already between her legs.

TWENTY-TWO

The next morning, they woke to find the forecast had been right.

The weather had suddenly improved, the sun was shining brightly, it was hot again, and there was no sign of the storm.

Weather wise that was.

Around them they could see the damage it had caused everywhere they looked.

As they walked out onto the balcony the next morning, Alina looked down at the garden and gasped in horror.

What had been a beautiful garden just a few short days ago was now a disaster zone. There were broken branches everywhere, plants had been uprooted, and there were even a few palm trees that had been downed by the wind.

As she stood there looking at it all Bear came up behind her, putting his arm around her.

. . .

"It's a bloody mess." He said sighing, "But we've been through this before. Once the important things are looked after Emanuel will have this done as well and in six months it will be hard to believe there was a storm, but unfortunately there's a lot of work to do before we get to that point."

He walked her over to the table where their breakfast lay waiting for them.

"At least it wasn't as bad as it could have been. Believe me I've seen a lot worse. That's just life on the island. You've got to accept it." He said, looking at her with resignation. "You just have to take the bad with the good."

* * * *

That morning he was going to the far side of the island to check on the sugar cane plantation and the rum factory, and Alina settled down once again with her book.

Now that the weather had improved, he'd ordered the plane for her and it would be coming in three days' time so she could be back in New York on Sunday, then return to work the following day.

Her time here would be over soon, she thought unhappily, *and she would miss it, but she needed to remind herself that regardless of how much had happened to her while she'd been here for just these few short days, this still wasn't her life.*

It was Bear's. Her life was in New York.

. . .

She knew now she loved him and she believe he loved her. Bear had been very serious when he'd said that to her, and he'd said it twice.

Yes, he loved her, she thought, sighing to herself, *but really, what difference would it make?*

His life was still so different from hers.

If she was lucky they'd get to see each other now and then, but in between there would be other women in his life and that was something she just had to face.

He had a huge sexual appetite, he needed sex twice a day, and he wasn't going to be happy without it.

When she wasn't there to give it to him, he would find someone else. That's what he'd always done, and even though she really did believe he loved her, it would be totally unrealistic to think otherwise.

That was who he was.

Besides, she told herself resolutely, *he totally wasn't the kind of man she really wanted for a permanent relationship anyway.*

His life was nothing like what she wanted, what she'd dreamt of having.

There were a lot of things about him she loved, he had a lot of great qualities, but he also had a lot that she hated and couldn't see living with.

The way he'd been when she heard him on the phone, so cold, so ruthless, that wasn't a man she could live with.

And he was very used to having any woman he wanted. That had never been and would never be a problem for him.

When he wanted variety, he could get it easily just by turning on that famous smile. In the end, regardless of what she did for him, she couldn't compete with that.

No, Alina thought with another sigh, *this man wasn't for her.*

The time she'd spent here had been amazing, making love with him would be very hard to beat, but it would be over very soon, and she just needed to prepare herself for that. Be realistic.

But she intended to enjoy it while she had it, Alina thought with determination.

After that last session had ended so badly Bear had been determined to never let things go that far again and he'd been true to his word. Making love with him was always amazing but he'd never come anywhere remotely close to the way he'd pushed her before.

As she thought about that, Alina remembered how good that first session had felt.

There'd been very little pain. Yes, there was some, but when you push yourself to your limits it's only to be expected. On the whole she'd definitely enjoyed it and she knew he had as well.

He'd really enjoyed it, and he'd told her he wanted that again.

· · ·

She would never want to push herself the way she had in that last session. That had been stupid and they both knew that now, but just because they'd pushed it too far was no reason why they should give up all together.

She knew he'd really enjoyed it, really wanted to have that experience again, and before she left she wanted to give it to him.

And if she was really honest, she wanted it for herself as well. Once she left, she wouldn't see him again until he came to New York and who knew when that would be?

She knew this storm had upset a lot of his schedule. He'd had to reschedule things around it, make alternative plans, and there was a very good chance it would be a long time before he could see her again.

I want to give him one more amazing night and give it to myself as well, and tonight I'll would convince him. she thought, determined now.

She really didn't want to have to leave him without having a chance to have that amazing experience one more time before she left.

* * * *

He finally returned late afternoon and joined her on the balcony where she'd spent most of the day. Sitting back with a sigh, he took a long swig of the beer he'd brought with him, then turned to her.

"Well, at least it's not bad." He said, sighing again.

"It's nowhere as bad as it was the last time, but there

will still be repairs that will need to be made." Then he smiled,

"But enough of that. I don't want to think about all that any more. Did you have a good day?" he asked.

"Yes, very restful." She replied, smiling, then she looked at him seriously.

"Can we talk about something?"

"Sure," he replied, looking at her with surprise. "What's on your mind?"

Alina took a deep breath. Would she be able to convince him?

She wouldn't know unless she tried.

"I know since that last session you've been restraining yourself. Your determined not to push me, not to cause me any pain, but Bear, I think you've gone too far to the other extreme."

He looked at her, obviously surprised.

"You do?"

"Yes," she said quietly looking at him. "I do. Trying to push it to an hour was stupid. And yes, there was a lot of pain at the end, but Bear, that was really just at the end. Most of it was amazing. I want to have that experience again, and I know you do."

He looked at her sheepishly then.

"I can't deny it Ally," he said looking at her seriously

now, "It was amazing, and I want it again. But not if it's going to cause you pain. It's not worth it."

Alina smiled.

"Remember the first time you pushed me? That was amazing, wasn't it?"

"Yes," he agreed, grinning now, "It was bloody amazing."

"Well there's no reason why we can't do that again. I want to do it for you. This is not just one sided you know. Just as you want to give me pleasure I want to give it to you as well. And this, this was amazing for both of us."

"It definitely was amazing for me." He said, still grinning, "and even though you were begging me to stop, in the end I could see you were enjoying it as well."

"Yes, I was. " She agreed, still smiling at him. He looked at her and she could see in his eyes that he really wanted this.

"Let's do it." She said quietly, and he grinned.

"God, you're a hard woman to please Ally," he said, "What can I say? If this is what you want, who am I to deprive you?" He was grinning at her wickedly now and she smiled back at him.

"Right." He said, still grinning, "No point in putting it off. We'll do it tonight. Already I can hardly wait."

As he sat back happily and took another swig of his beer, she smiled at him.

She'd been right to do this.

As she thought about it she felt those tingles starting again. The thought of it still scared her a bit, she had to admit. She was still pushing herself way more than she ever had before she'd come here, but she knew now she could do it.

She could give him this as her last gift to him before she left, and she would enjoy doing it.

In fact, she was looking forward to it as much as he was now.

TWENTY-THREE

That afternoon Bear left her for a few hours to work in his office, and when he came back, he grinned at her.

"God, Ally." He said, "I could hardly concentrate on my work. All I could think about was tonight. Now that I've had it, even though I was determined not to push you, I really wanted it again. I can hardly wait. It's been too long."

"Yes, it has." She agreed smiling back at him. "I've missed it too. We'll have to just make sure we do it more often."

"Sounds good to me." He said, smiling happily as he settled down beside her with another beer, and looked through the papers he'd brought out with him.

Alina smiled to herself.

This man was a total sex maniac, and now he'd turned her into one as well. Once he was out of her life she had no idea what she was going to do without it, but right now she was going to enjoy every minute of it while she could.

* * * *

Even though the damage the storm had caused was all around them, Bear was determined that life was going to go on as usual.

These storms were just part of life.

There was no reason why, once they were over, life couldn't return to normal.

He ordered the musicians again for that night and told her to wear the blue dress again.

"You look amazing in that dress Ally." He said, smiling at her. "I love looking at you all dressed up and thinking about what's under it. It's a hell of a turn on."

That evening when she walked out of her dressing room he was ready and waiting as usual, and as she looked at him she thought again how handsome he looked in that tux.

Whether he was all dressed up in a tux or standing in front of her in oil stained jeans and T-shirt it really didn't matter, she thought, *he was always handsome.*

As they walked out onto the patio she saw that all the broken pots had been removed and new flowering plants had been planted in all the containers. Bear greeted all the musicians again, then he led her to their table.

The dinner was amazing as always, and when they danced he held her tightly, kissing her neck, and she could feel how aroused he was already.

He's not going to want to dance long, she thought

smiling to herself, and she was right. After half an hour he'd had about as much as he could take.

"Time to leave." He whispered to her, his voice husky. "Now comes the part I've been waiting for all day."

As she walked into the bedroom, he was right behind her and as she stopped by the bed he was already unzipping her dress.

Taking off her underwear, he lay her on the bed, and standing over her, his eyes filled with hunger and need, he hurriedly removed his clothes.

After grabbing a condom, he took out the vial of pills again, and still looking at her swallowed a couple as before following them with water.

His preparations complete, he lay down beside her on the bed, and stroked her face.

"God, I want you so much Love," he whispered, then lowering his head he kissed her breasts, working his way to her nipples.

Soon she could feel herself getting wet again and as his hand reached between her legs he smiled.

Not wasting any more time on preliminaries, he thrust into her, making her come, and as before, he didn't let her come down, making her come over and over again as she moaned with pleasure.

Slowly, the more she came, the stronger the pleasure got and the more she craved it.

Her body couldn't get enough of him, welcoming him each time he thrust into her.

Again she completely lost track of time, but unlike the last time, there was no pain now, just pleasure.

Soon he was ramming into her hard, and still she wanted more. The feelings he created in her were so exquisite, so incredible, she never wanted them to stop.

It seemed to go on forever and still there was no pain.

Her moans got louder and louder, but they were moans of pleasure, and seeing that he just continued to make her come, over and over.

After what seemed like an eternity they started to get stronger. With each one she experienced more and more pleasure, her body vibrating with his every touch, and finally, sure she couldn't stand it any longer, her body trembling, she cried out.

"Oh God, Bear, Oh God!" then just when she felt she couldn't take it for one more minute, the feelings slowly started to diminish. She felt him thrust into her several times in a row, then moan as he came.

She was still laying there, trembling, completely exhausted, as she felt him move closer and softly stroke her face. Slowly she opened her eyes and saw he was watching her, looking happier and more content than she'd ever seen him look before.

. . .

"God, Ally." He whispered. "I thought it was amazing before, but that was unbelievable. That was forty minutes. And there wasn't any pain this time was there?" he asked, unsure now.

"No Bear," she answered him happily, "No pain, just tons and tons of pleasure."

He smiled happily then.

"It looked that way to me, but I wanted to be sure." Then he stroked her face again, his eyes soft with emotion.

"Being inside you when you were constantly coming for me for all that time, it was so fucking amazing I could hardly stand it."

Then he softly kissed her, and putting his arm around her she heard him sigh happily.

"There is no way I'm going to be able to live without that now. No fucking way."

The next morning, as he kissed her neck, he whispered softly in her ear.

"I can't believe after last night, I want you again so soon, but I do. More than ever."

His hand between her legs now, as his fingers felt how wet she was, he sighed happily.

"I love that you're always ready for me."

Moving with determination now, he made her come a dozen times, then finally came himself, and collapsed back onto his pillow.

As she turned towards him, still catching her breath, she looked at him.

He was lying there with his eyes closed, a smile on his face, and knowing that she'd put it there, made her day.

I might not have this man for long, she thought to herself, *but I'm bloody well going to make sure he doesn't forget me. And I'm going to enjoy every minute of it.*

TWENTY-FOUR

The next day he needed to check on the village again, and again he asked her to come with him.

She'd finished her assignment now and there really wasn't anything else for her to do, so she happily agreed.

She was also curious to see how the village had been affected. She'd met the people now, could see how much he cared for them, and she was starting to care as well.

As they drove along that same road, Alina couldn't believe how much it had changed.

There were broken branches everywhere, and here and there she saw piles of leaves mixed with paper and bits of other garbage, obviously blown there by the high winds.

"Yes, I know it's a mess," he said seeing her face, "But the nice thing about the jungle is that everything grows again so quickly. Meanwhile I've hired an extra work crew. They'll be arriving on the plane tomorrow. They'll soon put all this to rights again.

. . .

"Where do they stay?" she asked curiously. This was a private island after all and there were no hotels.

"There's a large bunkhouse on the other side of the village." He replied. "It contains a huge room with a dozen beds, a couple of bathrooms, a kitchen, and also a living area for them. I bring in a cook for them as well."

He looked at her and smiled.

"We still have lots to do here so it's constantly in use. As soon as things get back to normal, we'll start on the roads." He sighed then. "There's tons to do, but bit by bit it will get done."

Yes, I'm sure it will, Alina thought to herself.

He was so caring, so passionate about this island, and he obviously didn't think twice about spending his money here. No wonder everyone loved him.

They had tea again with Edwardo and Jimena, and after they ate, Emanuel took Bear aside and showed him some of his plans for the clean-up while Alina helped Jimena clean up.

Pedro and Chico were running around outside, happily playing, and as she watched them through the kitchen window while she dried dishes, she smiled to herself. '

This is what I want, she thought. *What Edwardo and Jimena have, this is what I want. But will I ever be lucky enough to find it?*

When they went to bed that night, he turned to her.

"I hate that this is our last night Love." He said, looking

at her sadly, "and God Ally, I want you so much again. I can't believe how much."

Then he sighed, "but after yesterday you need to rest. I don't want to push you. It's too much to expect it two nights in a row."

"No, it isn't." She said with determination. "It isn't too much. You've trained my body well Bear, and now my body knows it's limit. It doesn't push to the point of pain. It stops way before that. Let's just see how far it will go."

He looked at her and grinned.

"A week ago, I was saying that to you. Now you're saying it to me? I really have trained you well."

Then his eyes got that hungry look again.

"I guess now I can start to reap the benefits."

"Yes, you can." She whispered. "And I want you to."

He groaned and reached for her, kissing her passionately. His breath labored now, he made himself pull away. Getting out the vial of pills again he took his usual couple, then turned back to her, his eyes hungry with need.

His hand between her legs again, he withdrew his fingers and sucking them, he sighed with pleasure.

"God Ally, you taste so good." He murmured, "and you're always so ready for me."

Moving over her, determined now, he thrust into her, hard, making her come, and as he felt her body convulsing around him, his eyes closed with pleasure, then opening them again, even more determined now, he thrust into her again.

It was just the same as it had been the night before. All pleasure and no pain.

The pleasure just got more and more intense to the point where she felt she would faint from it, but it felt so amazing she never wanted it to stop.

Then, her body still reacting to him, she felt him come inside her.

She was completely exhausted now, but more satisfied than she'd ever felt in her life. Her eyes still closed, her breathing slowly returned to normal and after a few minutes she opened her eyes to see him lying beside her, looking at her, his face filled with contentment, his eyes soft with emotion.

"God," he whispered, "every time I think you've hit your limit, you haven't got any more for me, you give me even more. Forty-five minutes tonight. It's bloody amazing."

He softly stroked her face, his eyes on her still.

"You were still coming, but we know now the pleasure would have soon turned to pain. We're never going there again. We're never going over fifty minutes Ally, but God, it was fucking amazing."

"And all the time I'm fucking you I can feel how much you want me. God, it's such a turn on. The things you make me feel while I'm inside you. I've never felt like that before. And it just goes on and on. It's bloody amazing."

He was still stroking her face, but his eyes were serious now.

. . .

"I'm totally addicted to you Ally." He said, quietly. "I honestly don't know what I'm going to do when you leave tomorrow. I'll have to look at my schedule. I can't wait more than a few days before I see you again. I just can't do it. I've got to have this now. I've got to have you."

Kissing her softly, he cupped her body with his, and pulled the covers over them.

As she lay there waiting for sleep, still exhausted but incredibly content, she knew she would have a hard time living without him as well, but how the hell could it possibly work?

Then too tired to think about it any longer, she fell asleep in his arms.

TWENTY-FIVE

The next morning as she felt him kissing her neck again, Alina turned to him, smiling softly.

He was ready again but that didn't surprise her any longer. That was how he was.

He needed a lot more sex than the average person, and when she was gone she knew he would get it somewhere else.

That was how he was, but right now she wasn't going to think about that. Right now, she would just enjoy these last few hours they had together.

He didn't say anything more to her. Everything had already been said. He just looked at her, his face serious, and then he made love to her.

He was especially needy, determined to get as much as he could from her before she left, and after she'd come fifteen times for him, he finally came as well, then collapsed back onto his pillow, totally exhausted, his breathing still labored, his eyes closed.

After a minute he opened his eyes and turned to her.

"I love you Ally." He said quietly, "I really do." Then stroking her face, she heard him sigh as he turned away and with resignation started to get out of bed.

After their usual breakfast out on the patio, Bear gave her a kiss and then left for his gym. The plane would be there early afternoon and she needed to finish her packing.

As she was still sipping her coffee, her cell rang, and she looked at it, surprised. All the time she'd been here nobody had called her. There had really been no need.

Answering, she heard Gerald on the line.

"How's my favorite writer doing?" he asked, and she could picture him sitting smiling at his desk.

She'd been working for him for five years now and they had a very good relationship.

In a lot of ways, he'd been her mentor, teaching her the business, helping her when problems arose, and she admired and respected him. Up until this assignment she'd done everything he'd asked of her very willingly and never questioned his decisions, knowing that he always had her best interests in mind.

He knew that she wanted this promotion, knew that she

was ready for it, and hopefully he'd give it to her, but she had to admit the competition was pretty fierce.

There was one man in particular who was just as qualified, and she knew Gerald was considering him seriously as well.

She'd just have to see how it all panned out, she thought with a sigh, as she answered him, doing her best to sound happy and cheerful.

"Great. It really is beautiful here. How did the series go over?"

She knew he'd released it several days ago and she was anxious to know what kind of feedback he was getting.

"Very, very well." He said, obviously happy. "Amazingly well in fact. That's why I'm phoning. I don't want you back in the office next week Ally. I want you to stay where you are and work on some new assignments."

As she listened, surprised, he slowly explained.

"The series went over very well and now there's a lot of interest in Bear and his island. National Geographic wants an article and they're sending a photographer. There are a couple more magazines that want one as well. One's a business magazine, and I think that's what finally made Bear agree."

"He's always been very protective of his privacy. I don't know how you got him to agree to publish what you wrote, but it's started something now. Something big. It's going to make him much more famous, it's going to be a major win for us as a company, and it's going to make you Ally."

· · ·

She heard him sigh.

"Look, I know you didn't want to do this. Bear insisted he wouldn't work with anyone else and I know you weren't happy about it, but you have to admit it's worked out very well. For some reason he's opening up to you and we have to take advantage of that. Bear's agreed to all these other articles, even to the photographer, but there's one condition."

At this point Gerald stopped and sighed again.

"He will only work with you Ally. He wants you to stay there on the island with him for the next couple of months until these are all written and he's adamant about it. He said you did a good job and he doesn't trust anyone else to portray his work."

"Look Ally, I know you're not happy about this, but it's the only way he'll cooperate, and this is going to be major for us. I told him that, of course, it was up to you. You've already done a great job on that series. If you're not prepared to stay there any longer I won't demand it. But I am prepared to bribe you into staying," he said, and she heard him laugh.

"I know you've got your eye on that promotion. If you do this, if you stay there for another couple of months and get these written, that promotion is yours. What do you say?"

At that point there was a silence and Ally knew she had to decide quickly, but she also knew that her decision was already made.

If she could stay here with him for that much longer there was no way she would turn it down. The only question was if Bear would get tired of her. As far as she knew he'd never stayed with any one woman this long in his life.

Was he likely to change now?

Not bloody likely, she thought with a sigh, but still she knew she had to stay.

When she told him, Gerald was ecstatic.

"You won't regret this Ally," he said, obviously relieved. "This is all going to work out marvelously."

She wasn't all that sure that was true.

Yes, he wanted her now, but another couple of months? That was really pushing his limits and she knew it.

As she was sitting there still thinking about it, Bear walked through the door, and sitting down opposite her, he looked at her anxiously.

"I gather Gerald called you."

"Yes." She replied quietly.

"I have to admit I was surprised when he called me. And I'm still not really sure all these articles are such a good idea." He sighed then. "But if it means I'd have you for longer, then there really was no other choice for me to make."

"So, what did you tell him Ally?" he asked her quietly.

"I'm staying. Of course." She said, looking at him, "But Bear, why? I know you don't do long term. You never get involved with anyone for more than a few weeks as far as I can gather. Why are you doing this now?"

"I told you. I love you." He replied quietly, looking at her seriously.

"With you, I want to try." Then taking her hand he kissed it, still looking at her.

"I want to try Ally," he said, looking deep into her eyes, "And if it's at all possible, I want to make this work."

He smiled, and she could see his mood change.

"I've got to go make some calls. See you later Love." He said, still smiling to himself as he walked back out the door.

TWENTY-SIX

That morning Gerald had all the information she would need emailed to her, and as she looked through it Alina had to admit that she was excited to do this.

Yes, it would definitely make her name just like Gerald had said, but it would also give her a chance to write more on the island.

People had obviously enjoyed what she'd written in the series and wanted to know more, and she was more than willing to satisfy their curiosity.

She knew she would have to be careful.

Not give away more about his private life than was necessary.

He wasn't really comfortable with people knowing too much about him and she had to respect that, but there was still so much she could write that would definitely portray him in a good light and she was anxious to take on the challenge.

. . .

Once she'd spent an hour in the library setting up her files on her laptop, Alina decided to take a break and go out onto the patio and read. It was a beautiful day again and she wanted to take advantage of this great weather while she could.

She knew now how quickly it could change, how easily the hot days could turn to cold, and she wanted to sit out in the sun while it was out.

She would have a couple of months now and she could build up her tan.

Settling herself in a chair she started to read. She was engrossed in a particularly interesting chapter when again she heard Bear's voice from the other side of the patio. It was even louder than it had been before, and his voice carried clearly.

"Damn it!" he exclaimed, and his voice was cold and angry. "I warned that man. He knew what would happen if he screwed me."

There was a short pause, then she heard him say.

"Do it. Get it done today and let me know when it's done." Then obviously having hung up, she heard him mutter,

"That fucking bastard. I'm going to teach him a lesson he'll never forget."

She heard him slam something down on his desk, then the door slammed as he obviously walked out of the room.

Fuck, she thought to herself, *this man is bloody scary. I definitely wouldn't want to have him as an enemy.*

The ruthless way he seemed to treat people when they crossed him made her feel cold.

Was anything really that important?

She'd never known anyone who controlled so much money and had so much power, and the thought of what he was capable of when he was crossed sent cold shivers down her spine.

This was a man who was totally different from the one she knew.

He was cold, calculating, determined to have his way, and it sounded to her like he was willing to go to extremes to get it.

Could she seriously get involved with a man like him?

He was completely different from the man she'd pictured in her mind that she wanted.

That man was loving, caring and compassionate. Yes, he certainly had those qualities as well, she'd seen them for herself, but this cold ruthless side of him was something she didn't know if she could live with.

If she ever did anything to upset him would he turn this mean vindictive side on her as well?

That wasn't something she ever wanted to find out, but in every relationship, there were always disagreements.

There were always things that would need to be worked out between them, and if he was always going to be so determined to have his own way it would never work.

. . .

I can't think about this anymore now, she thought to herself with a sigh. If I think about it too much I won't be able to stay with him any longer, and she knew leaving would never really be an option for her.

She had to see this through to the very end.

Just as he'd pushed her with her orgasms, she had to push herself with him.

Regardless of what happened with their relationship, regardless of how much heartache there could be for her once it finished, she knew she had to see it through to the end.

I need to think about something else, she thought to herself resolutely, and as she remembered the last time she'd had tea with Emanuel and Jimena she remembered their talk.

While she was in the kitchen with her, she'd asked Jimena about her work at the school.

"I love it." Jimena had said, turning to her with a happy smile, but then her face changed. Looking worried she continued.

"I love it but it's getting to be too much. We have so many more children and I just can't give them all the individual attention they need.

I wish I could, I really do, but it's just not possible. I know Bear is trying to hire someone else for the next year until Valentina finishes her training, but he's finding it almost impossible.

Nobody wants a temporary job, especially not here." She said sighing.

She looked at Alina and smiled again.

"But somehow I'll cope. This is still a lot more than we had before Bear took over. We'll find an answer."

"So, you need another teacher?" Alina had asked, curiously.

"No, she doesn't have to be a teacher," Jimena said, sighing again, "Just someone with a good knowledge of English and a bit of math will do.

These are young kids. The curriculum isn't that involved. I'm just trying to teach them some basic skills. In a North American school, they have parent helpers and that works very well, but here ... well most of the parents are uneducated themselves.

Before Bear came they had no school so none of them even learned to read or write."

As she sat there going over that conversation in her mind, Alina thought again about an idea she'd had.

After returning with Bear that night she'd realized she wanted to help, but she was leaving so there was no way she could.

Now she would be here for another couple of months. The work she needed to do didn't take up all her time by any means. She could easily help Jimena.

She certainly had all the skills. Why not?

She'd gotten to love these people just as much as Bear did.

They were simple people and they lived very simple lives, but the ones she'd met were warm, caring and loved their families.

As far as she was concerned these were traits she'd

always admired, always valued a lot more than business success and making tons of money, and she really wanted to help them.

That evening at dinner she talked to him about it.

"Bear, I know you've had problems getting someone to help Jimena. You still haven't been successful, have you?"

"No, he'd said," sighing. "But I'm not going to give up. There has to be someone out there."

"How about me?" she asked.

He turned to her in surprise.

"You? You've already got a job. You have all these articles to write. And you're not a qualified teacher, are you?" he asked.

She realized then that he really didn't know anything about her background. Didn't really know anything about her family, her friends, her life.

They'd been too busy with other things to spend any time talking she thought, sighing, *but soon she would have to change all that. If he was really serious, if he really wanted to try and have some kind of relationship with her, then, much as it was amazing, they needed more than just sex.*

Getting her mind firmly back on the topic she looked at him, her face serious.

"No, I'm not a qualified teacher Bear, but I do have a degree in English and three years of college.

Jimena says she doesn't really need a qualified teacher. An educated helper will do."

. . .

She looked at him, anxiously.

"I'm going to be here for another couple of months. It's not the year you need, but it will fill the gap for now, give you time to find someone.

What do you say? I want to help. I really do."

He looked back at her thoughtfully, then slowly smiled.

"You really want to do this? Your schedule will be very full if you take this on you know."

"So is yours," she answered him, laughing.

"Doesn't seem to bother you. And I'd like the challenge."

He kept looking at her, then she saw in his eyes he'd made up his mind.

"Okay." He said, still smiling, "If you really want to do this Ally it will be a big help.

I need to drive down to the village again tomorrow. You can come with me. We'll drop by the school and you can talk to Jimena while I finish up some other business."

Then his mood changed and he smiled at her, wickedly now.

"I thought it would be a good chance for us to go swimming again. Thankfully the pond wasn't touched by the storm. But this time no bikini." He said, his eyes twinkling.

"We'll swim nude. That will definitely turn me on, and there will be less for you to take off for what follows."

Then still smiling, he took a drink of his wine, and she

could see by his face he was looking forward to it with eager anticipation.

That night when he made love to her he again seemed content with pushing his own limits and didn't take the pills even though she'd told him she was quite willing to push herself for him.

She was addicted to him just as he'd said he was addicted to her, and she was also addicted to that feeling of intense pleasure she always had when she was coming for him.

"You're going to be here for at least the next couple of months with me Ally," he'd said with a smile.

"And much as I'd love to do this every night, I'm not going to wear you out. I want you to be able to do this for me as long as you're here with me, and if you're going to do it, much as I'd love to push you I know now it's stupid."

Then he'd smiled that wicked smile she'd grown to love so much.

"You're going to rest for a day or two in between. Just pushing to my limits is enough. It's a hell of a lot more than anyone else has ever given me. We'll do it two or three times a week." He'd said smiling, "The anticipation will make it even more pleasurable."

That certainly was sensible, Alina knew, but she also knew that if he'd want to push her to her limits every day she was with him she would have done it until she no longer could, and the thought really scared her.

Was she really so addicted to this man?

What the hell was going to happen when all this ended?

Because she was sure it would.

Much as he'd told her he wanted to try, he was used to constant sex, constant variety, and much as he'd said he loved her, at some point he would miss it again, want someone other than her.

She knew that, had told herself that over and over again, but it was still difficult for her to imagine any kind of future without him now.

The longer she stayed with him the more and more hooked on him she became.

TWENTY-SEVEN

The days seemed to pass quickly after that, but with Bear there was never any routine.

Many days he would start the day in his gym, then work in his office, but for just as many days his routine would change completely.

Sometimes he left very early, his business taking him to the far side of the island, and other days he would skip the gym all together, spending most of the day on his phone.

As she'd known would eventually happen, he told her one evening he needed to go to New York on business.

He would be gone for three days, but she couldn't go with him because the photographer was due to arrive the next day. His plane would be depositing him on the island before taking Bear North to New York and she needed to meet with him.

She was also committed now to helping Jimena at the school and she wasn't going to let her down.

. . .

Ally knew this would be a major test for their relationship.

This man had a ferocious sexual appetite and he wasn't used to doing without. Would he find someone in New York to fill his needs?

Probably, Alina thought with a sigh, *and she honestly didn't know how that would make her feel.*

She believed he loved her now, but she also knew he would want sex and she wouldn't be there to give it to him, so it would only be natural for him to find someone else to fill his needs.

She expected that, had known that it would probably happen and had told herself she would just have to accept it, but whether when it actually came to it she could, she honestly didn't know.

She knew that in places such as France, a man playing around on his wife was perfectly acceptable.

They looked at sex and love as two different things. Sex was just filling a need.

But could she do that?

It wasn't what she was used to, wasn't what she'd grown up seeing with her Mother and Father, and she very much doubted she could, but she would have to try.

If she wasn't prepared to do that, she might as well tell him that she wasn't interested in a relationship with him, wasn't interested in trying, and that it could never work.

Unless she was prepared to accept him for who he was, there was no chance this would work.

. . .

But could she do it?

That was the million-dollar question, Alina thought to herself with a sigh, and thinking about it she knew that until it actually happened, until she found out that he was sleeping with another woman again, she would never truly know.

* * * *

Jimena had been thrilled when she had offered to help her, and when Alina walked into the small school house for the first time she could definitely see why.

The tiny building was crammed to the rafters.

Bear had told her that there were plans to build an addition in the coming months, but meanwhile they had to make do and there were a lot of students and very little room.

Thankfully, because of the constant sunny hot weather, a lot of the classes could be held outdoors.

The small school house was on a large lot, surrounded by several groves of palm trees, and sitting under them as the giant fronds rustled in the soft breeze that seemed to be a constant companion, it was very pleasant.

One thing they didn't have to worry about was supplies. Bear had made sure of that.

He had made it very clear to her when he'd first talked about it to her that educating these kids was a high priority for him and he spared no expense. The cupboards on the far wall might be tiny, but they were crammed with notebooks, pencils, pens, crayons and markers, and all kinds of other equipment.

There was also a large bookcase on one wall filled to capacity with school books.

Whenever Jimena mentioned she could use something, Bear bought it for her, and as she started her first day working with the students Jimena had assigned to her, Alina marveled again at his generosity.

He could be so thoughtful, so caring, so loving. But as she remembered the conversation she'd overheard the other day she knew that he could be cold, ruthless and vindictive as well.

Which was the real him?

Would she ever know?

Or was he actually both?

It was very possible, Alina thought, *and if that was true could she live with a man like that?*

She had no idea.

Even though the sex was amazing, she loved spending time with him, and really didn't want to leave him, she still thought that when it came down to it she probably would.

Living with a man like him would be amazing and also horrible at the same time.

Could she put up with both of these very different sides of his character?

Who knew? she thought with a sigh, but she had a feeling she would soon find out.

She didn't know how she would be able to deal with the cold ruthless businessman or even if this side of his life would affect her, but the other women? She had a feeling she would have an opportunity to find out soon enough how she felt about that.

This was a man who needed sex twice a day and he was going to be in New York for three days.

The chances of his going without it, especially since there were so many beautiful women more than willing to oblige him, were slim to none and she knew it.

She would just have to see how she felt when it happened. Find out if she could handle it, or if it would end up being a deal breaker, and sadly, she knew the latter was more than likely going to be true.

* * * *

The children she was assigned were very young as Jimena had told her they would be.

They were all five or six years old and were often accompanied by a parent when they arrived at the school.

One day, as she was filling out some forms at the teacher's

desk, Alina noticed a young woman, probably in her late twenties, standing by a young boy who was on her list.

Mateo was a lovely little boy, bright and cheerful, and she enjoyed working with him. As she got up to speak to his mother, she noticed her picking up one of the books from the desk by Mateo and leaf through it, a wistful look on her face.

"Hi." Alina said, determined to befriend her.

It was important that the parents supported their kids and wanted them to get an education, but she didn't need to worry about that she soon found out.

The woman looked up from the book and softly smiled at her, but she didn't say anything.

"I see you're looking at Mateo's textbook," she said to her with a smile. "This is what they are learning right now."

The woman still smiled but her eyes were sad.

"Would you like to borrow any books for yourself?" Alina asked her.

She knew there was a well-stocked library in the back room of the school, and Jimena encouraged those who could read to borrow the books.

"I would love to," the woman answered quietly. "But I can't read. I'm glad Mateo is learning. His father and I didn't have the chance to learn when we were young. There was no school then."

She looked wishfully at the book.

"I wish I could know what it says."

Alina smiled at her sadly. she really didn't know what she could do to help. She was only here for a few months.

* * * *

That evening, after she'd finished the writing she'd scheduled for that day she decided to do some searching on her laptop.

Now that Bear was gone, it was a great opportunity for her to get ahead of schedule and she'd worked several hours in the couple of nights he was gone, but she couldn't work more than a few hours each day.

After that she found her creativity dissipating and writing became harder and harder. It was much better to put in a few good solid hours, then to let her mind rest and move onto other things while the ideas built again for the next day's session.

Tonight, she wanted to look into adult reading classes.

She really didn't know anything about that whole area, but it seemed to her this was something that was just as badly needed here.

Yes, educating the kids was important. That's what they needed so they could improve their lives, but shouldn't the adults have a chance at some education as well?

Now with the Internet there was so much they could learn online, but to do that they needed to be able to read.

As she checked various websites, she found that there were a few dedicated to online classes.

There were programs that people could follow at home and teach themselves.

This didn't seem very possible to her, but as she checked them out and looked at a few sample lessons she saw that they were very straight forward and even if you couldn't read you could follow easily.

Instead of written instructions the instructions were all audible. The student could work through each lesson, listening to the instructions, and at the end of the course they would have the basic skills and be able to read.

Of course, it would help to have someone there to help them, to guide them when they had problems, but it wouldn't require a lot of time.

A teacher could set them up and then just check on them occasionally after that. The lessons were very easy to follow and the more she looked at them the more excited she got.

The one she liked the most, only cost a few hundred dollars, and for a couple hundred more, you could get a license for up to ten computers.

As Alina sat and thought about it she remembered that Jimena had shown her the laptops Bear had provided for the school.

There were ten brand new ones, and right now only a handful of older students were using them. Why not make them available to some of the adults as well?

She was going to be here for a couple of months.

She could easily start them on the program, and if she was willing, Jimena could just answer any questions they had. Most of the time they would be able to work alone, so it wouldn't take up much of her time.

* * * *

Excited now, Alina talked to Jimena about it the next day. As she listened quietly, it was hard to see how she felt about it, but once she had finished, she looked up at her, and Alina could see she was smiling.

"Oh, Alina, that's a great idea!" she said, excited now as well. I'm sure Bear would happily buy the program. As soon as he comes back I'll ask him."

"We don't need to wait for that," Alina said to her, smiling back. "I'm going to buy it for you. This will be my gift to the school. I'm busy just as you are during the week teaching the kids, but on Saturday I'll spend a few hours setting up a class. I can get them started and help them with any problems they have while I'm here."

"You'd really do that?" Elina asked her in surprise. "This isn't your responsibility. I'm sure Bear will be happy to pay for it."

"Yes, I'm sure he would be as well," Alina answered, determined now. "But I want to do this Jimena. I'm only going to be here for a couple of months, but I'd still like to help as much as I can."

. . .

Jimena looked at her and she could see her eyes were glistening with tears. She took her hand, her face filled with gratitude.

"That would be great Alina. Thank you." Jimena said, her voice breaking.

"Before Bear nobody cared. We got used to it. To see you actually do. It's ..... Heartwarming? "She said, laughing now. "Is that the right word?"

"Close enough." Alina answered, tearing up herself.

This woman's gratitude was overwhelming.

"Close enough."

TWENTY-EIGHT

Bear was going to be away Thursday, Friday and Saturday. He had some functions to attend he'd told her, then he would return on Sunday.

It was Saturday, and as she sat on the terrace having her breakfast, her cell phone rang again.

Picking it up she was surprised to hear Jimena.

"Oh, Alina." She said, happily. "You'll never believe it. You know I asked all the parents to let me know if they were interested in learning how to read. Well nineteen have already said they are and wanted to know when you would start the class. Isn't that amazing?"

Alina agreed. It really was amazing.

"I can set up two classes Jimena," she said, quickly. "One this morning and one this afternoon. Maybe three hours each?

What do you think?

Then next week they can come in again and I'll supervise. Bear is always busy doing something or other during the day. If he needs the jeep he can drop me off."

"Or Emanuel can." Jimena replied,"and he can drive you back. But today? Are you ready?"

"Sure." Alina replied. "Bear left me the jeep to use and I don't have any other plans."

Other than writing she thought, but she could easily do that when she got back. It wasn't like she had anything else to do.

"That would be amazing." Jimena said, "I'll let them all know."

* * * *

Alina quickly went online and paid for the program then downloaded the trial version for herself.

She was only going to be there for a couple of months, so that would work for her. She wanted to keep the ten versions on the license for the adults to use. Sounded like there were a lot of them ready to use it.

Navigating the pot filled road was definitely a challenge, Alina thought as she drove towards the school, but it definitely beat walking and she knew most of the natives still had to walk from place to place.

There weren't many cars on the island, but as usual, Bear had provided enough.

Along with his own he'd also bought one for Emanuel to use, there were several more available to whoever needed them and could drive, and there was also a bus that was used to transport the work crews.

Again, Alina marveled at Bears generosity and thought how really wealthy he must be to be able to afford all this. She'd never known anyone who had that kind of money and it certainly took some getting used to.

He was definitely using his wealth to do good, she thought, *but if he'd had to be cold, ruthless, uncaring and vindictive in order to accumulate it was it worth it?*

This was a question she couldn't answer.

She had expected at least ten students, but she was amazed when she finally reached the school. Jimena was already there, signing people up on a clipboard she held in her hands.

"Looks like we'll have to have more classes." She said smiling.

"I'm starting a waiting list. When the first groups finish I can start some more. This was an amazing idea Alina," she said again, smiling happily.

Alina had never taught anything like this before and she was a bit anxious, but it all went very well.

Jimena had set up the laptops on a couple of large tables, and she quickly got the program loaded on each one, then after she had worked it out for herself, she told them exactly, step-by-step how to start.

. . .

The class was mainly women but there were also several men, and they all were very keen.

As she sat there supervising them and working through the lessons herself so she would know what they included, she was amazed at how keen they all were.

They were all determined to learn and excited at each accomplishment, chatting happily among themselves, then returning once again to the laptops.

The three hours she'd allotted went by amazingly quickly, and as she went around to each one to see how far they had managed to get she really was amazed.

They had all progressed through the programs with ease, and even though there had been a few questions, nobody had any major problems.

It had gone very well, and she congratulated herself on how well, as she stood in the doorway watching them happily walking back to their homes, talking and laughing with each other.

Emanuel came and picked up his wife and they both insisted she return with them and have lunch. The break between her classes wasn't that long and Emanuel had already made them some sandwiches.

As she sat and joked and laughed with them on their patio, the scent of the flowers above them filling the air, and Pedro and Chico happily playing on the lawn next to them, Alina thought to herself again how much she envied them their relationship.

· · ·

This really was what she wanted.

Was there even a chance of having anything even remotely like this with a man like Bear?

As she thought about his cold ruthless side, about all the women he needed, she very much doubted it.

Yes, she wanted to try, and she would, but was it going to be enough?

Somehow, she didn't really think it would be and the thought saddened her.

The afternoon class went just as well as the morning one had done, and once it was finished Alina drove back to the house feeling very pleased with herself.

She knew she'd made a difference in these people's lives. She'd experienced just a small amount of what Bear must feel every time he thought of how much he'd done for these people, but even that small amount had been deeply satisfying.

As she walked back into the library, Melinda followed her in with a tray.

"I heard about the classes you're holding Missy." She said with a smile. "That's a very caring thing for you to do, and it's made a big difference already. Everyone is talking about it."

Alina smiled back at her. That hadn't really been her goal, but it was nice to be appreciated.

"I brought you some tea." Melinda said as she put the tray down on the table.

"And the New York paper. Mr. Bear orders it in every day but he's not here now and I know you're from New York so I thought you might like to have a read and catch up on what's happening in your home town."

As Alina thanked her, she smiled at her once more and went back to her kitchen.

Alina was planning to write for a couple of hours but holding all those classes had been tiring and she could do with a bit of a break.

There were a few comfortable chairs on the far side of the room, and she settled herself in one of them with her cup of tea by her side and began to read.

She'd made her way about halfway through the paper when she came upon the society pages and saw Bear's photo prominently displayed there.

He was wearing a tux and smiling into the face of a very beautiful brunette. He had his arm around her and the brunette was smiling up at him. Underneath the photo the caption read.

"Playboy Billionaire and his Latest Conquest."

As Alina looked at the photo she started to feel cold.

He'd told her he had functions to attend but he'd never mentioned he was attending them with another woman. A very beautiful one at that who obviously knew him very well. And he certainly seemed happy to be with her.

. . .

Well, Alina thought to herself, *this was what she'd expected to happen wasn't it?.*

This is what he'd always done and even though he'd told her he loved her, and they had just spent over three wonderful weeks together, obviously that hadn't been enough to make him change.

Here was the evidence, staring her right in the face.

He still needed other women in his life, would probably always need them, and he wasn't likely to change.

Slowly she folded the paper and placed it in the trashcan. Somehow, she no longer felt like reading.

Alina slowly sipped her tea.

Well now it had happened. She'd known it probably would, had told herself that was what he was likely to do, but now that she knew that he actually had, could she accept it?

Even though she'd thrown the paper away, the image of him standing with that woman, his arm around her, smiling into her face, was imprinted now on her memory, and it wasn't likely to go away anytime soon.

Could she live with that?

Could she ignore it?

When he came back and reached for her again, could she make love to him, knowing that only hours ago he'd left some other woman's arms?

.   .   .

As she sat there thinking about it, Alina knew that she couldn't.

She loved him.

She didn't want to share him.

Couldn't bear to share him.

Reading about his other women and trying to ignore them would be total hell.

She couldn't do this, she thought. *This wasn't the kind of life she wanted. The kind of man she wanted.*

She was here now, and she had promised to stay for a couple of months, so it wasn't as if she could just leave.

She needed to stay, to finish these articles, so she could make sure she got that promotion. Make sure she had something to go back to when she left. Because she knew now she would leave.

She loved him, and she had to stay, so while she was here she would just have to suck it up.

Not sleeping with him would be impossible.

Even though she knew now he was totally the wrong man for her, that she would need to leave him, she was here, and while she was here she would have to make herself do it. Make herself act normally, pretend she didn't know, ignore it, and enjoy their time together.

Because it wasn't going to last.

She knew that now, had no idea how she would deal with leaving him, but she would.

She had to.

. . .

Meanwhile she would enjoy it while she could, enjoy every moment they spent together making Love, then once she left she would block him from her mind forever and never allow herself to think about him again.

This man was dangerous.

She'd always known it, yet she'd allowed herself to want him, to love him, and now she would have to pay the price.

TWENTY-NINE

When Bear returned the next day, Alina was determined she was going to act as if nothing had happened.

This was how he was, how he would always be, and she had only two choices - to accept it or to leave him - and that second one she knew wasn't really an option.

She made herself greet him with a smile, sit in the living room and ask him about his trip, and stay away from anything to do with that woman.

He didn't bring it up either, and all the time she talked to him it was on her mind, but she knew there was no point going there.

He wasn't going to change.

He went off then to the library to leave some information she'd asked for on her table, and as she sat there thinking about it Alina realized that ignoring it was the only thing she could do.

This man was never going to change.

At this point she didn't think he could, and she couldn't expect it from him. He might want to try and make their relationship work, but she knew now that would never happen.

While she was here with him she would make herself ignore all his other women and just concentrate on him and how he made her feel when he was with her, but once this assignment was over she was leaving.

Hard as it would be now to leave him, to forget him, she knew she had no choice.

She couldn't live with this for the long term. It would be much too hard to take.

She would end up hating him just as much as she loved him and eventually it would drive her crazy.

That night when they went to bed Alina made herself act normally.

They'd had a nice dinner on the terrace as usual, and she'd made herself laugh and talk and listen, not letting herself think about it any longer. As long as she was with him this was going to happen, probably over and over again, and there was no point in expecting anything different.

But it was always there.

He'd been with someone else in New York, she'd seen the evidence in the paper, and try as she might she just couldn't ignore that.

He'd looked at her with those dark eyes of his at dinner, and she'd known he knew there was something wrong, but he hadn't said anything.

As he took off her clothes and lay her on the bed, she wasn't really sure this was going to work any longer.

She still wanted him, still wanted how he made her feel, but now she also knew he wasn't just doing it with her. There was someone else, someone who would probably step in to fill the gap when she was gone, and even though she still believed he loved her, she wasn't enough for him.

Probably never would be.

He took of his clothes, his eyes constantly on her face, but this time instead of reaching for a condom, he came and lay down beside her, and stroked her face. Just looking at her, then finally he sighed.

"Do you want to tell me what's wrong?"

No, she didn't, she thought, *what was the point?*

But instead of waiting for an answer, he answered himself.

"I can see you're not going to tell me, so I'll have to tell you." Then he looked away and sighed.

"It's that bloody newspaper article with the photo isn't it." It wasn't a question.

He knew.

. . .

Turning to her, he looked at her seriously.

"I saw it in the library trashcan by the table where you work. I know you've seen it."

She still didn't know what to say. She just really didn't know how to talk to him about this without getting emotional, and that wouldn't help anything.

Sighing again, he spoke softly, his voice low and caring.

"I wasn't with that woman Ally," he said quietly. "She's Daniel's wife."

Then seeing she had no clue who he was talking about, he sighed again.

"We're obviously going to have to have a serious talk soon about our families and people we know, otherwise these kinds of misunderstandings will keep happening."

He was still looking at her, his hands now stroking her hair.

"Daniel's my broker. He and his wife are good friends. Cindy and I went to her charity ball together because Daniel had the flu. And really didn't feel up to it. She'd been working on this ball for ages, and it was really important to her, so I offered to step in for Daniel and take her."

Then sighing yet again, he looked at her sadly now.

"I never thought about how it would look, honestly, I didn't. I knew these bloody papers are always taking photos of me with women, but I just didn't think."

"I'm sorry love." He said quietly.

"I wasn't playing around on you. I don't want to. No other women appeal to me anymore," then he looked at her ruefully.

"And that makes business trips very hard to take. You know I have a very healthy sexual appetite. For me, I need it twice a day and I've never had any problem finding someone who will fill that need. You know that as well."

He stopped then, and still looking at her whispered softly.

"I love you Ally. You're the only one I want. I don't want anyone else."

He was thinking about something, his face unsure, then making up his mind, he continued.

"Much as I wanted it, and believe me I wanted it, you weren't there to give it to me. So, I had to take care of my own needs." He said, sighing.

"I haven't had to do that since I was about twelve. I wasn't at all sure it would be enough, but I just thought about you in bed, coming for me, all the time I was doing it, and it worked." He said, grinning now.

"Definitely not as good as the real thing. But a hell of a lot better than sticking it into someone I really had no desire to be with."

Then he looked at her, his face serious.

"Do you believe me Love? He asked softly.

"I know I have a horrible reputation, but I swear to you it's true. You're the only one I want now."

. . .

Alina looked at him. Was this really true?

This man who could have any woman he wanted had actually abstained?

Masturbated instead?

It was really hard to believe, but looking at him, at the look in his eyes, she suddenly knew that it was true.

He loved her, and the fact that he was willing to do this for her was no small thing.

He'd never been willing to do it for anyone else and knowing that made her love him even more.

"Yes," she said smiling softly at him, "I believe you."

"Good," he said, "because I haven't been with anyone else since I've met you Ally. I haven't wanted to be, and if this is what I have to do when you're not there..." he sighed once again, "then I guess this is what I'll have to do."

Then as always, his mood changed just as quickly as it had appeared.

"Now can we get to the sex already? I don't know how much longer I can wait."

"Okay," she said smiling happily, but when he turned towards the drawer to get a condom she stopped him.

"No. You don't need that." She said, determined now.

"I trust you. I trust you're not lying to me. If you haven't been with any other women since you met me, then I think it's safe. It's been almost a month now. I think it's safe.

I've been on the pill for years, so you don't need to worry about birth control either. You don't need to use a condom any longer. It will be much more pleasurable for you without it."

He looked at her, surprised.

"No condom? Are you sure Ally? I've always used one ever since I started having sex. To be honest I've never done it without one."

"Well then," she said, still smiling at him, "I think it's time you tried it. You're the one who's always pushing me to have new experiences. Don't you think it's time?"

Then she added quietly.

"Take the pills tonight. You've got a lot of catching up to do."

He just looked at her, then he grinned.

"God, I love you so much Ally," he said, still grinning. Then turning resolutely towards the nightstand, he opened the drawer and swallowed the pills.

It was amazing as always, but this time, it was even more amazing.

And not just for him but for her as well.

There was so much more feeling, and it was so much more intense. Even though she would never have believed it was possible, the feelings were so incredible it made her want it even more than before.

. . .

Again, it seemed to her the pleasure went on forever, and when he finally came, she again lay in his arms, exhausted.

As she finally opened her eyes she found him lying on his pillow, looking at her, obviously completely exhausted as well, but grinning, a very satisfied look on his face.

"Bloody hell!" He said to her, "It's always been amazing, but this .... I can't tell you how fucking amazing it felt. The feeling was so much more intense. There were moments I thought I was going to pass out it was so intense.

I had no idea it would make so much difference. I've never enjoyed sex this much in my life. Never, and believe me I have a lot to compare it to!"

Then he stroked her face, his eyes filled with love as he looked at her.

"God, I love you so much Ally. You're constantly surprising me." He said softly.

With a happy smile still on his face, he cupped her body within his, drew the covers over them, and his arms around her still, with a happy satisfied sigh he settled down to sleep.

THIRTY

The next morning, like always, he was ready again, and even though this time there were no pills, he managed to last until she'd come twelve times for him, and again, he lay back with a happy, satisfied sigh.

"God, that was good!" he said grinning, "I might have to go to three times a day."

Then looking at her horrified face, he laughed.

"Don't worry Love," he said, still laughing, "My mind might want it, but my body has its limits."

Sitting on the patio again having breakfast, he turned to her, smiling.

"So, what's the plan today? Are you at the school again?"

"Yes," Alina replied, "Do you need the jeep?" she was getting used to the roads now, so the drive no longer worried her, but she knew he always had places he needed to go.

"Yes, I probably will." He said, still smiling, "But I've had one of the other ones driven over here for you to use.

Obviously, you're going to be needing it every day now. The keys should be on the table in the hall.

As they chatted and she caught him up on what had been happening, telling him about the adult reading classes she'd started, he stared at her admiringly.

"You are constantly surprising me, you know that? " He said, then he looked at her anxiously.

"I hope you're not overdoing it Ally, he said," concerned.

"Will you still have time for your writing? I don't want Gerard on my back."

"Don't worry," she answered, laughing. "I've got it all worked out with Jimena. I'm just starting them off, then she's going to take care of the rest. This program is very easy for them to follow and when I was with them nobody had any trouble following it. I'm sure it's going to work out really well."

"Yes, I'm sure it will." He said, smiling at her again.

The next few days passed quickly. Now that he was back, that she was no longer worried about what he was doing when he wasn't with her, she could concentrate on her work at the school and the more she got into it the more she loved it.

She'd met some of the older students now and she was very impressed with how well Jimena had planned their studies. There were four girls and six boys in the senior class and they were all planning on continuing their education. Jimena had prepared them well, they had all gotten good marks on the college entrance exams, and they were excited to be going to the States to finish their studies.

Bear had flown them to Miami in his jet when they

had to write the tests and made it available for them when they had decided on the schools where they wanted to apply, putting them up in hotels for a few days so they and their parents could check them out before the classes started.

One of them was studying to be a dentist, another one was studying pharmacy, and several of the girls wanted to become Nurses.

Bear happily paid all their expenses, and the only thing he wanted from them was a promise that once they got their qualifications they would put in three years of work on the island.

After that, if they wanted to move somewhere else they would be free to go, but all of them had family here, they loved living on the island, and it was very likely that the majority would stay, which would allow the island to grow and expand even more.

Already Bear had plans. He wanted to expand the clinic, make the pharmacy bigger, and as planned the school would soon be twice its original size.

This must all be costing him a hell of a lot of money, Alina thought, but he talked to her about these plans with great excitement and seemed to be more than willing to pay for it all.

She knew that without having the vast sums of money he obviously had there was no way any of this could have happened, but she still wasn't sure the cold, hard man he'd obviously had to become had been worth it.

She knew she could never have done it, but then she wasn't Bear. When she thought about it she had no idea what his background was, what was really driving him, or how he really felt about his work. Did he enjoy it or was it just a way to make money? She had no idea.

One day very soon, she thought, *she would have to talk to him about it.*

The following week Jimena asked her to help the older class with their English assignments and as she read over their work she noticed that several of them were very good writers.

She'd had another idea, and when she talked to Jimena about it while they were having a break, sitting outside enjoying the sun and drinking mineral water from the large fridge that Bear had provided for the school, Jimena laughed.

"You're definitely getting into all this, aren't you. You'll miss it when you leave I think, just as much as we'll miss you."

Alina had decided to help them start up a village website. One where they could share news, information and other things the village would find useful, and the kids she'd been helping were the perfect ones to start it.

It would give them some great practice using their writing, and when they left to go overseas to school, the kids that took their place in the class could keep it going. It would be great for all the adults now that they were learning to read, and great experience for all the kids as well.

When she told Bear what she was doing, he'd just smiled without commenting, but at the end of the week when his plane made its weekly drop of supplies, a couple of huge cartons were delivered to the school, and when she and Jemina unpacked them they found along with the other supplies that Jimena had asked for that Bear had also ordered another two dozen laptops.

"They are for your Adult's class Ally," he'd said when

she asked him about them. "I don't want the parents to have to share with the kids. This will make it a lot easier for them. Once they've finished the course and can read, Elina can give each one a laptop as a graduation present. They can take them home with them since there is Internet all over the island, I've made sure of that, and they can continue to read and learn."

As she'd thank him, she marveled again at his generosity. He didn't just provide the basics, he provided much more, wanting to make sure everyone had more than they needed, encouraging them to grow, to expand their minds, learn what they were capable of doing, and this warm, loving caring side of him was the side she loved.

Maybe it would be enough, she thought. *Nobody's perfect. Yes, there are a lot of things about this man I don't like, but there are also a lot I really love. Maybe it will be enough.*

THIRTY-ONE

Sunday was the only day Alina wasn't at the school now, and after breakfast, when Bear had left her to go to his office, telling her he had an appointment, she decided to once again go out onto the patio and read.

It was, as usual, a hot sunny day, and as she settled herself down with another cup of coffee Alina smiled happily to herself.

Things really seemed to be going along well.

The photographer's visit had been a great success and he'd managed to take a lot of amazing photos. She'd met with him before he went out with the man who'd been assigned to drive him around the island, and they'd discussed what photos she would need to showcase her article.

She'd talked about it with Bear before he left, and he'd told her where he was prepared to let him shoot and what areas were off limits and she'd stuck to his wishes.

The man who drove him around the island had been given the same instructions, and the man only saw what Bear was prepared for him to see.

That was a lot and she wasn't complaining, but some of the areas he'd designated as off limits had surprised her.

For instance, there was a whole section at the Northern tip of the island that he wouldn't allow him to visit.

He'd told her that it wasn't necessary for him to see it, that what he would be able to visit was enough, and certainly it was, but she'd wondered what was up there that was such a secret.

But even though she was curious, Alina hadn't asked him.

If he wanted her to know he would tell her, meanwhile she wasn't going to pester him with questions he obviously didn't want to answer.

But still, she was curious.

The day had gone very well, the photographer had left very pleased, and Gerald had told her the article she'd submitted for the magazine had been very well received.

She'd also finished the couple of other ones she'd been asked to write, and other than a few small pieces that she still needed to finish, there really wasn't that much more for her to do, which was good, Alina thought.

She could concentrate on working at the school and

with the Adult classes, and this was really what she wanted to do.

While she was here she wanted to help as much as possible.

Relaxing, she was getting into her novel again, when again she heard voices coming from Bear's office, and again he was angry.

His voice was colder than she'd ever heard it, even in the other two conversations she'd overheard, and she looked up, listening to the conversation, horrified.

What she was hearing was turning her blood cold.

"You've been stealing from me." Bear said, his voice cold as ice. "You've been stealing from me and you knew what would happen."

She heard a man's voice then, pleading.

"But Bear, you don't understand ...."

"No!" he roared, and his voice was louder than she'd ever heard before.

"You're the one who obviously doesn't fucking understand. You knew what would happen, but you did it anyway. Now you're going to suffer the consequences. Pack your things. The boat will be coming in the morning and you and your family will be on it."

· · ·

"But Bear ..." the man pleaded again.

"Don't call me Bear!" he roared again, "only friends call me Bear. It's Mr. McCalister to you. And I don't want to hear any more.

They will come to pick you up at seven, and once you're on the boat, Emanuel will give you your last check. You should be bloody thankful that you're getting anything. You don't fucking deserve it."

Then before the man had a chance to reply, he roared at him again.

"Now go, before I change my mind and just be thankful I'm as lenient as I am with you. You deserve a hell of a lot worse and if I didn't feel sorry for your wife and kids I'd make sure you got it."

"Go!" he roared again, and a minute later she heard the door close behind him.

"Fucking bloody Bastard." Bear said, obviously alone again, then she heard him slam the door behind him, but this time he headed out onto the patio, and a minute later he came into view.

She was standing now, her book forgotten, unable to move.

This man who was walking towards her was nothing like the one she knew.

His face cold, devoid of all feeling, he walked quickly,

and when he saw her he stopped. Then looking at her, his face still unchanged, he spoke.

"Fuck." He said, still looking at her, his face totally emotionless, "I need a drink."

A minute later he disappeared into his living room and she heard him remove the cork from the bottle and the clink of glass.

Shocked and stunned, when she was finally able to move again, Alina sat down once again on her chair.

Shit! She thought, *this man is a monster.*

How can there be such two different sides to him?

How can the warm, loving, compassionate man she knew and loved, have turned into someone so cold, unfeeling, and vindictive?

She picked up her book. There was no way she was going back in there.

He was angrier than she'd ever seen him, and she didn't want him to start turning that anger against her.

The best thing she could do was stay right out of his way, but as she tried to put her mind again on her book she found it was totally impossible.

She was shaking.

How could she even consider staying with this man?

She would be scared every single day wondering when that anger would be directed at her.

She couldn't live like that.

She must have sat there for over half an hour, her coffee now cold and untouched, her book in her hands but still closed.

Finally, she stopped shaking, and as she turned her mind with determination to her book once more he walked out, sitting down in the chair opposite her.

Slowly she put the book down again and looked at him.

He was holding his drink and he'd calmed down, but his eyes were still angry. Then as he looked at her they slowly started to soften.

"I'm sorry you had to hear that Ally," he said finally, sighing. "But sometimes these things have to be done. That's just the way it is."

"Do they?" she asked him quietly.

She knew she was taking a chance on making him angry again, but she no longer cared. There was no way she could hear something like this, know that he knew she'd heard him, and not say anything.

He looked at her for a long time, then he sighed again.

"Yes, they do." He answered, quietly now, his anger completely gone.

"I deal with a lot of people, handle a lot of money, and have a lot of responsibilities. Responsibilities that would take too long for me to explain to you. I believe in treating people fairly. I give them good working conditions and I pay them what they are worth. Nobody has anything to complain about."

"But there is one thing I will never abide and that's dishonesty. I'm an honest man, it's something I value above all other qualities. I'm an honest man, and I will never, never put up with lying, cheating or dishonesty of any kind from any of my employees."

He was looking at her seriously now, and after a minute he continued.

"Everyone who works for me knows that, and they know exactly what to expect if they ever go there. Diego was cheating. He was stealing money from the store profits, pocketing it for himself, and cooking the books. That's something I will never, never put up with."

Then he stopped still looking at her, and added quietly.

"I don't put up with dishonest people. I might have a lot of traits that aren't all that admirable, but dishonesty is not among them and never will be, and I will never put up with it in anyone else."

Seeing she wasn't going to say anything, he got up and looked at her again.

"I have to go out now. I won't be back for a couple of hours. When I get back I'd just like to pretend this never happened."

Giving her one last look he walked back into the living

room and a minute later she heard him put down his glass on the table, then walk out of the room.

Fuck! She thought.

She probably shouldn't have been surprised, especially after having heard him before, but never the less she had been.

Surprised and scared.

How could he possibly expect her to pretend it had never happened? She couldn't see that ever happening.

* * * *

When he finally returned, he'd completely calmed down, and he smiled at her, acting as if the incident had never happened as he'd told her he would.

He asked her about her day and she made herself answer him as normally as she could, but she still watched him cautiously.

As they sat on the terrace that evening having dinner he was his usual charming self, and when they walked back up to the bedroom, he walked up to her as she stood looking down at the bed and kissed her neck.

Slowly he removed her clothes then lay her on the bed and took of his own, his eyes never leaving hers. He was still serious, still looked determined, but she could also see the hunger building in his eyes once more.

As he lay down beside her and reached for her, again kissing her neck, Alina wondered if she could do this.

Make love to this man who she now knew without a shadow of a doubt had this ruthless, vindictive side to him?

She didn't know if she could go through with it.

As she was lying in his arms, her head filled with doubts, he slowly lifted his eyes and looked at her, then stroked her face gently with his fingers.

"I'm not perfect by any means Alina," he said softly, "I've never pretended to be. I know there are things about me that you find hard to take. But I love you, and hopefully that's enough. If it isn't I don't know what else to say."

"This is who I am. I'm not going to change. If you want me you'll have to accept me for who I am. As I've told you, I'm an honest man. I'm never going to lie to you.

I love you Ally. I want you more than I've ever wanted any other woman in my life, but I'm not going to make promises I can't keep.

Ever.

I hope to God you want me enough to accept that."

Then he lowered his head, kissing her breasts, his hand between her legs now, softly stroking her, and as he slowly made love to her she found herself responding.

Even though she'd really thought it wouldn't be possible, that seeing that side of him would completely turn her off, it hadn't happened.

The more he made love to her, the more she wanted him, and that night she came for him a dozen times. As he lay back, spent, his eyes closed, she turned and looked at him.

This was her fate now, she thought.

Regardless of all his faults, she still loved him, still wanted him, and even though she hated the side of him he'd shown her today, she knew this was never going to change.

THIRTY-TWO

The next day was Monday and as she worked at the school, sitting at her desk, watching the children working on an assignment she'd given them, she thought about what had happened the previous day.

She'd known when she'd agreed to try and make this relationship work that it would be hard.

The sex was amazing, she wanted him as much as he wanted her, and they were totally compatible in that area, but as she'd told herself before, for a relationship to work there had to be more between them.

They had to find out about each other, their families, their friends and about their work, but also their dreams, what they both wanted in life, what they loved, were passionate about, and whether or not they were compatible in those areas as well.

. . .

She loved the warm, generous side of him, but the cold ruthless side would be very hard to live with, regardless of how much she loved him, and as she thought about it she wondered how much more she was going to find out about him, and whether when she did, it would be good news for them or bad.

She didn't have long to wait to find out.

It was a half day today, Jimena was going to spend the afternoon talking to the parents at a parent/teacher meeting she'd set up, and Bear was coming to pick her up.

As she got into the car, he smiled at her and kissed her.

Things were back to normal between them now. When it had first happened that fight she'd heard him have with the store owner had caused a lot of tension between them, but after they'd gone to bed, had made love, it had gradually disappeared.

He'd made love to her again the next morning as usual, and even though she would never forget it, she'd gradually made peace with that whole incident, and seeing that, she could see him gradually relax again.

He was obviously thankful that she'd been able to accept it, had loved him enough to accept him for who he was, and she had, that was true.

But that didn't mean she was all that sure she could do it long term.

That would be a whole different thing.

. . .

He drove happily down the road, but instead of heading in the usual direction he took her further up the coast, and she turned to him in surprise.

"We're not going back to the house?" she asked.

"No," he replied, grinning at her, "It's time I showed you my favorite way to relax, after sex that is." He'd added with a wicked grin.

"I haven't had much of a chance to go out since you've been here, but I've missed it, and it's too perfect a day not to take advantage of it."

As he talked she noticed he'd driven her into a small marina.

There were several small boats tied up and bobbing in the water by the dock, but what took her breath away was the large sailboat tied up beside them.

"This is Millie." He said, laughing, "I know, crazy name for a boat, but that's what my grandfather named her. My grandmother's name was Mildred. While they were alive they both loved sailing, and since I inherited it I've found I love it as well."

"In fact, it's become a real passion for me. Going out on the water, feeling the wind on my face as it blows through the sails, it's the best way I've found to relax. I certainly could never give it up now."

They'd parked by the boat, and as he turned to her she could see his eyes had lit up with excitement.

"Come, I'll show it to you." He said with pride.

As he led her onboard, Alina followed him cautiously.

Sailing? She'd been on boats a few times, but she'd never really liked the experience.

She just wasn't comfortable on the water, she thought with a sigh, *but if it meant so much to him she would have to try and learn to enjoy it. As he'd said, he wasn't going to give it up any time soon.*

Even though she hadn't expected it to be, Alina found the afternoon was very enjoyable. She knew this would never be her favorite thing to do, she would never be as passionate about sailing as he obviously was, but if it made him happy she was willing to go out with him.

He was obviously a very good sailor, had maneuvered them expertly around the island, and they'd stopped by a beautiful beach to eat the lunch that Melinda had packed for them.

Then he had taken off his clothes and jumped off, laughing, and daring her to join him, and she'd found their swim very refreshing.

It was actually a lot of fun, she thought happily, *still not her favorite thing to do, but she could think of worse.*

As she lay in his arms that night after they made love, she realized she'd enjoyed the whole afternoon much more than she'd ever expected.

The island was beautiful, he was an expert sailor, and the boat was fully equipped, even luxuriously so.

It wasn't huge, with just a small kitchen and living area with one bedroom below deck, but all the built-in furnishings were sleek, modern, and obviously expensive as well as very comfortable.

He'd told her he'd take her on an overnight trip on the weekend, so they could try out the bed and even though he'd grinned at her wickedly, obviously anticipating it with pleasure, she wasn't all that sure about it, but she was willing to try.

It had been beautiful out today and going by the good weather they always seemed to be getting these days, there was a good chance it would be beautiful again on Saturday.

Jimena was going to be supervising the classes, so she could easily take the day off. How bad could it be?

* * * *

The day had dawned hot and sunny. When he drove them to the little marina again, there was a light breeze blowing.

"Perfect day to be going out." He said, smiling happily at her, obviously looking forward to going out again.

She just looked at him and smiled.

It was true that he had a lot of stress in his life. This would never be her favorite pastime, but if it allowed him to relax for a while and forget all the cares and responsibilities he had to deal with on a regular basis then she was happy to go along.

Well, maybe not happy, she thought, *that would be pushing it, but definitely willing.*

They had a wonderful day, sailing out on the open water

now, leaving the island far behind them, and even though she'd looked at him unsure when she'd seen it receding further and further from view, he'd just smiled.

"Don't worry Love," he'd said, I know what I'm doing. I've done this for years, and this boat is as safe as a boat can be. It has all the latest equipment and is totally water tight so if it was ever necessary to ride out bad weather, there wouldn't be any problem in this."

She'd smiled back at him, and even though she did believe he knew what he was doing, she still didn't feel all that comfortable.

And I probably never will, she thought to herself sighing, *I'm just not a lover of water like he is, but since it obviously makes him happy I'm willing to try.*

As evening approached, the winds got stronger, and he went below to check the forecast. As he came back up the stairs she noticed his face had changed. Even though he still didn't look worried, he looked a bit concerned.

"Looks like there's a storm coming. "He said, sighing, "and we're really too far out to get back to the island now before it hits. Go on down. I'll lock everything up and be down to join you soon."

Then seeing the worried look on her face, he added softly.

"Don't worry Love. There's nothing to worry about. Regardless of how strong it is we're perfectly safe in here. You couldn't find a safer boat."

As she walked down to the kitchen below she still could feel the anxiety building within her.

Safe? In a storm? How could they be safe in a storm?

She would rather not find out, she thought, sighing again, *but it looked like she wasn't going to have any choice.*

True to his word it wasn't very long before he joined her, and sinking down on one of the kitchen benches, he looked at her.

"We're pretty much ready for anything now." He said, smiling, "Let's have some supper."

As she ate the chicken stew Melina had prepared for them and drank her wine, she laughed and joked with him and made herself act normally.

This is obviously no big deal. She told herself sternly, *He's been through these kinds of storms before.*

She knew this was true.

When they'd returned home the first time he'd taken her out sailing, he'd told her how he'd often gone out with his grandparents, how he'd sailed for years in the summers with his friends while he was going to College, and how he'd made sure he got out as often as he could ever since.

Yes, there had been storms he'd admitted, but nothing this boat couldn't handle, and looking at his confident face, she'd made herself believe it was true.

He knew what he was doing, she told herself with determination *and he's done this for years. Nothing would happen to them.*

But deep inside she was still starting to get afraid.

The wind was getting stronger and stronger now, and

even though he'd put away everything after they'd eaten so nothing would be thrown around, she still wasn't amused by the way the boat was now being tossed about.

There's nothing fun about this anymore, she thought, *but what's the point in worrying?* It was too late now to do anything but ride it out, and she might as well make the best of it just as he was doing.

They'd finished the wine with their dinner, and she had to admit she was feeling very mellow. At least as mellow as she could under the circumstances, but there was nothing much she could do to help that.

"Let's go to bed love." He said getting up with a grin. "I know just how to help you relax."

He'd brought his pills with him and as he made love to her in what she had to admit was a very comfortable bed, Alina started to feel herself relax.

If nothing else this will certainly take my mind of it, she thought, as he moved over her, and it definitely had.

For almost an hour the pleasure was all she could feel and everything else was forgotten.

Now that he wasn't using the condoms any longer, they were both enjoying it even more than they ever had before, and she was just as eager for him as he was for her. When he finally came he fell back with a sigh of contentment.

"Fuck. it just gets better and better." He said, smiling happily. "Your amazing Ally, I love you so much."

Drawing her body against his, he settled down content-edly to sleep.

The wine and the sex had done its job, and totally relaxed now, she fell asleep in his arms, sleeping soundly through the night as the boat tossed and turned in the turbulent water.

They slept deeply, lulled by the rolling waves, and when they woke up she could see the sun streaming in through the little window.

As she lay there, slowly waking, she realized that the tossing and turning had stopped.

The boat was still rolling in the waves, but the motion was gentle and pleasant now, and as she opened her eyes she felt him kissing her neck, his body ready for her again.

I guess he was right, she thought to herself as she turned to him smiling, *we've managed to get through it safely.*

But later, when she was laying in his arms as he lay beside her, his eyes closed and a contented smile on his face, she knew this would never be one of her favorite activities.

He loved it, it was a big part of his life, and if she was going to be part of that life she would have to learn to love it too, but even though she knew she would probably get used to it after a while, she would never feel as passionately about sailing as he did, and when he went out without her, especially when the weather turned stormy, she would always remember the storm they'd weathered and worry until he returned.

He would never give this up.

He was passionate about it and sailing would always be a big part of his life, but could she live with the worry?

Yet another thing to consider.

They loved each other passionately, the sex was always amazing and that was a major plus, but she was also finding more and more things that she didn't especially like about him and his life, and to be honest, really wasn't all that sure she could live with.

THIRTY-THREE

Since that last conversation, Alina had been thinking long and hard about what she'd heard.

She still hated the way Bear could be so cold and uncaring, how scary he was when he was so angry, and she did wonder if one day he would turn that anger onto her.

She'd never known a man like him, had no way of really gaging his reactions, no way of knowing what to expect, but she did believe he loved her.

And she'd promised to give this relationship a try.

He was very secretive in a lot of ways.

She was slowly learning a lot more about him and the life he led now after having spent so much time here, but she still felt there were a lot of areas that were off limits to her.

A lot of topics he skirted, a lot of questions that were unanswered, and she knew that if they were going to have any chance of deepening this relationship, any chance of having it last, then they would need to open up to each other, to trust each other, and she also knew it was up to her to make the first move.

By his own admission, Bear had never been in a long-term relationship before. He had no idea how to approach it, had no experience opening himself up, and she would have to lead the way.

Determined now, Alina turned to him one morning while they were having breakfast.

It was, as always, a beautiful day. The sun was shining brightly, the new flowering plants that had been planted in the patio pots were quickly growing, and the scent of the flowers was all around them.

He sat relaxed, content after their morning sex, sipping his coffee. There would be no better time.

"Bear, can we talk?" she asked as he turned to her in surprise.

"Sure. What's on your mind?"

Looking at him lovingly, but also slightly anxious now, she made herself continue.

She'd had a very happy childhood it was true, but just like everyone else it hadn't been perfect.

Just like everyone else her family had experienced its

share of problems, and she wasn't any keener to talk about them then he was, but this needed to be done.

"I told you I'm going to try to make this relationship work just as you've told me you want to try as well. In order to do that we have to get to know each other. Open up to each other."

He was still looking at her, but his eyes had that guarded look she'd seen too many times before.

With determination, she continued.

"This is not easy to talk about. On the whole, I know I was very lucky. I grew up with two very loving parents, a mother and father who loved us all and also loved each other. They had a wonderful relationship, still do after all these years, and gave us all a wonderful example."

"We never had a lot of money. We were comfortable, but certainly not rich. My father owned a hardware store before he retired and sold it, and he enjoyed his work.

He's a very outgoing man, always friendly, always happy, and people loved to come in just to chat with him. He's kind and compassionate, very optimistic, and is never very serious, preferring to enjoy life rather than worry about it, but he's also in many ways a very wise man."

"My mother is the ultimate Martha Stewart," she said, smiling to herself as she thought about her. "Even though she never had tons of money to spend she knew exactly how to spend it well.

Our home was always comfortable and inviting, always

beautifully decorated, and when it came to holidays she always outdid herself.

She and my father live in Florida now and she doesn't do much of that any longer, but we always had amazing holidays while we were all growing up."

"As I said, we never had a ton of money, but our parents were determined that we would still enjoy life. In the summers, we would spend our vacations camping. There were several National Parks in our area, several fresh-water lakes, and we took full advantage of them.

I remember spending a lot of time swimming and hiking, and often Dad would take us fishing. There is nothing like the taste of freshly caught fish cooked over a campfire." She said, smiling at him now.

"At Christmas, our house was always decorated, always filled with the scent of gingerbread men or other cookies, and all my brother and sister's friends as well as mine loved to come over.

Mom was always friendly, always smiling, and she made them all very welcome.

We never had a ton of gifts, but there was always one big gift for each of us, and we never really missed out on anything. We made gifts for each other, and sometimes they were very weird, but we all had a great time together, and crazy as the gifts might have been, we always knew they'd been made with love"

"On Halloween Mom spent hours making us incredible costumes, then she and my Dad would go out with us.

While we went from house to house collecting candy, they would stand on the street watching us, talking and laughing with the other parents. It was a very happy, very loving home, and I always felt very blessed."

"I have an older sister and an older brother.

Jessica is great. We're only a few years apart in age and have always been very close.

It was wonderful growing up with an older sister, sharing things together, and even though we didn't always get along and certainly had our share of fights, we were always very close.

She works in New York as a designer now, and we meet every couple of weeks for lunch.

She's engaged to a great guy. He's a banker and he's very like my Dad, friendly, light hearted, and each time I see them together I can see how much he loves her. They're planning their wedding for next spring."

She stopped then and looked at him. He was just looking at her thoughtfully, looking for all the world as if the kind of life she described was totally foreign to him, and she wondered again what kind of childhood he'd had.

Hopefully, once she opened up to him, he would open up to her, but first she had to tell him the rest, and this was the hard part.

Alina swallowed, then continued, looking up at him seriously now.

"But it wasn't perfect Bear. Like all families we had our share of problems."

He was still looking at her thoughtfully, and she could see she had his full attention now.

"I also have an older brother, Paul. He's always been a rebel. He's loving, charming, and smart as a whip, but following rules was never his strong point."

She took a deep breath then and looked at him.

She knew now how strongly he felt about honesty. He was adamant about it. Would he be able to accept this, or would he judge her, judge her family?

If he couldn't understand, then having any kind of relationship would be pretty much impossible.

She loved her family, loved her brother, even though he was far from perfect, and she couldn't live with a man who couldn't accept him.

She was taking a risk here, she knew, but it was a risk she had to take.

Taking another deep breath, she continued.

"Paul was always getting into trouble. As a small kid, he drove my parents crazy. He was always disobedient, would never follow directions, and got into one scrape after another.

Once he became a teenager it was worse. He started to hang out with the worst crowd at school, went to a lot of wild parties, and many an evening I'd watch from the top of the stairs as my father walked in the door with him, supporting him, while he stumbled into the house, drunk.

My parents were worried, I knew that, but he never did anything really bad. Until one day."

Alina took another deep breath. Now that it came down to it she didn't know if she could continue, but she knew she had to try. He was still looking at her, not saying anything, and with determination she carried on.

"As I said, he got in with a bad crowd. One night the police came knocking on our door. He and his friends had been caught stealing booze and cigarettes from the corner convenience store.

It was late at night, there was only a young girl running the place at the time, and even though they hadn't hurt her, she'd been scared, and as soon as they walked out of the door she called the police."

"We lived in a small town. Everyone knew everyone else, and everyone looked out for one another. My father was well-known, a well-respected member of the community, and I could see the embarrassment this whole thing was causing him.

It was very hard for him to take, but he dealt with it very calmly, and even though at the time what he did seemed very harsh, it ended up being the right thing to do."

"My brother was just sixteen, my father and the store owner were good friends, and he didn't press charges, so Paul didn't end up with any kind of record, but my Dad had had enough."

"He banned the kids Paul had been hanging out with from our home. Paul bitched and complained, but my Dad was adamant.

All that summer he made Paul work in the store stocking shelves, giving all the money he earned to the owner to pay for the things he and his friends had stolen, and that fall he sent Paul away to military school."

"My mother hated it. Even though he was a constant source of pain, she really loved him, and I heard her crying one evening as my Dad tried to talk to her about it.

My Mom never cried. Believe me, that conversation stuck in my mind forever."

"He spent three years at that school, returning only on vacations, and even though it cost my Dad a lot of money, money he had to take from our vacation budget and his retirement savings, he was determined to keep him there, and it ended up being the best thing that ever happened to Paul."

"He changed completely. Each time he came home for vacation it was more and more evident. He grew to love it there, love the friends he made there, and believe it or not, the Air Force is now his career.

He's a fighter pilot now, and my parents still worry about him every time he goes out on a mission, but now he's turning his rebellious side to something worthwhile."

Alina stopped then and looked at him. She was sure this was all very different from the rich privileged childhood he'd probably enjoyed.

Would he be able to understand?

Bear was still looking at her, but his eyes were warm and loving. He turned to her and taking her hand he held it softly, stroking it gently.

"Thank you for telling me Ally." He said quietly, "It sounds to me like your Father's a very loving, as well as a very smart man. Fathers should all be like him."

Then he got up, walking over to her and kissing her softly on the forehead.

"I've got lots of work I need to do. I'll see you at lunch." He said, then still looking thoughtful, he walked out the door.

Well, he seems to be okay with it, Alina thought to herself, but his reaction was still guarded and she still really didn't have any idea of how he really felt.

I've done what I could, she thought with a sigh, *I've opened up to him and it was bloody hard.*

Would he be able to do the same?

She could see when he left that he'd obviously taken

what she'd told him very seriously, that he needed to think about it.

Would he finally trust her enough to open up to her as well?

Sighing again, she knew that now it was all up to him. She would just have to wait and see what he did.

THIRTY-FOUR

The next morning, after he'd made love to her, after they had both gotten up, she was heading for her bathroom when he called her back.

He was still sitting on the bed, his face serious.

"Come sit by me love." He said quietly. "I want to talk to you."

As she walked over to where he sat and sat down quietly beside him he took her hand, holding it softly with his.

"You told me a lot about yourself yesterday Alina, and I appreciate how open and honest you were. I think it's time I was just as honest with you."

He was very quiet now, and Alina waited while he sat there, quietly gathering his thoughts. Then he turned and looked at her.

· · ·

"We all have secrets Alina," he said quietly, sighing, "And often they are very painful. Things we don't want anyone to know. I have my share."

"What I'm going to tell you now. Very few people know." Then he looked at her and she could see the love in his eyes.

"I've never wanted to share this with anyone, but if we're going to make a go of this, build some kind of relationship together, then we need to be totally honest with each other. You were honest with me yesterday and I know that wasn't easy for you. Today I'm going to be honest with you."

As she sat there looking at him, he looked deep into her eyes, then obviously having made up his mind, he looked away.

"This is a long story. It started many years ago. When I was born in fact."

He looked back at her and she could see how deadly serious he was.

"I was born into a very rich family. To the outside world it looked like I had been incredibly lucky, that I had more than anyone could possibly need or want, but that was far from the truth."

"What very few people know and will never know is that I have a twin brother. Randall Bernard McCalister the third."

He looked at her and smiled.

"I know, it sounds crazy, but my grandfather wanted us

both to be named after him, so we were. The order of our names was just changed."

As he looked away, obviously thinking about him he softly smiled.

"Randy's an amazing person. Kind, loving, gentle, and always happy."

Then he sighed.

"He's also got a huge amount of problems. Has had since birth. His brain didn't develop properly and neither did his body. He's always going to have the mentality of a five-year old, and he has to live his life in a wheelchair."

"But he had at least developed as much as was possible, and that's only because my mother took such good care of him those first few years. She wouldn't allow my father to send him away. She insisted he stay with us at home."

He was silent for a long time before continuing.

"She died when we were six. My father was a cold, unfeeling man. He insisted on keeping his existence secret. Even though I often had my photo in the papers with my parents, Randy was never included in any of them. Very few people knew he even existed."

He stopped again, and Alina could see how hard it was for him to talk about this, but after a couple of minutes he continued on with determination.

"Once my mother died, everything changed. My father wasn't a family man and the last thing he wanted was to be saddled with a couple of kids, especially when one of them wasn't normal."

"He sent Randy to a home and me to boarding school. He enjoyed his easy-going carefree life, enjoyed doing whatever he wanted, and was determined that was never going to change."

"I very rarely saw him after that. Every vacation and holiday I spent with my grandparents, and even though they were good people, they really weren't much better at providing a family life."

"They'd never had one, growing up in boarding schools just as I did, and even though they were kind and generous, living with them was never like having a true home."

"My grandmother tried. She really did, she was a wonderful lady and I have a lot of fond memories of her, but I definitely didn't grow up with the kind of family life you've told me about. "

He sighed and looked at her.

"That kind of family is something I've never known."

Looking away he continued.

"During all those years I kept in touch with Randy. My grandmother would take me to visit him whenever I was with her, and she went to visit him often as well, but the place he was living - well it definitely wasn't anything like a home.

It was very well run; my father spent a lot of money

making sure he was sent to the best he could find. But in the end, it wasn't a home.

The people who took care of him were kind and compassionate, but they didn't really care for him. He was just an inmate.

He never had any love from anyone. Other than when I or my grandmother visited, he never saw anyone who really loved him."

He took a deep breath, and she saw a look of determination cross his face.

"I was determined that just as I was going to help these people here, somehow I would get him out of there, and once I bought this island I did. I had a house built for him on the far side of the island. It's large and spacious and right on the beach."

"I've also hired a couple to take care of him. They're a married couple, Jenna and Andy, in their late forties now, and I had a home built for them as well right next to Randy's."

"They are really wonderful people, both of them have nursing training so I know they can handle anything that might come up, and they take care of him very well.

More than that, they seem to really love him now, and more than anything, that's what he needs. What he's missed all his life."

He stopped and looked at her, his face serious.

"A lot of times when I tell you I have to go to the far side of the island on business, that's where I go. I try to see him a couple of times a week, and he's always a joy to visit. I'd love to have him here with me, but I know that's not really practical."

"I don't live a very settled life as you know. I never know when I will have to be away, what will come up, and I often have visitors. I don't want to expose him to all of that. He's much happier where he is and more than anything I want him to be happy.

He already has so much to deal with in his life. The doctor's say a man like him won't live very much longer. His internal organs haven't developed fully any more than his arms or his legs. But whatever time he has, I want him to be happy."

He was looking at her searchingly now, and she leaned over, kissing him softly, her eyes full of tears.

He had lived through such a horrible childhood, had never really known a happy loving home, and her heart was breaking just thinking about it.

How had he managed to endure it?

To make himself go on never having any support?

The strength that must have taken was unbelievable.

"I love you Bear," she said softly. "I am so sorry. So very sorry. I can't even imagine what your childhood was like. What you've been through since then."

. . .

He smiled at her then.

"Yeah, it was tough. But it's things like that, that show you what you're made off. It wasn't great, but it made me stronger. That's even more reason why I'm so determined to protect what I have. I've had to work too bloody hard for it, a lot of people depend on me, and there is no way I can let them down."

Then he looked at her anxiously.

"Can you understand that Alina?" he asked her quietly. "I know I seem cold and ruthless to you at times, but it's the only way I know. The only way I know to protect the people I love."

She leaned over and kissed him again.

"Thank you for telling me Bear." She said quietly. "I know this wasn't easy for you to do."

Then she looked at him questioningly.

"Next time you go see Randy, will you take me with you? If you don't feel comfortable doing that I'll under-stand. I know how hard this must all be. But he's your twin brother. He's a big part of you, an important part of your life, and I'd like to get to know him as well."

Bear looked at her, still very serious, for a long time, then he softly smiled.

"I'm going again in a couple of days." He said, "You can come with me if you like."

"I like," she whispered softly as she kissed him once more, and when he kissed her back, passionately now, with a growing need building in his eyes, she kissed him back just as passionately.

He lay her down on the bed then, making love to her again, and as she loved him back she could feel her heart expanding even more.

Was there ever going to be an end to all the amazing things she found out about him?

She already loved him more than she'd thought was possible, but still, the more she learned about him, the more that love grew.

THIRTY-FIVE

The day they were going to visit Randy was hot and sunny as always, and as they drove in the jeep down the rut-filled roads, the sun beating mercilessly upon them, the cool wind that blew softly around them, was very welcome, blowing through their hair and cooling their skin.

The house Bear had built for Randy was on the most Northern tip of the island, the area where he'd forbidden the photographer to go, and now Alina knew why.

And I don't blame him, she thought. *With the kind of reputation, he had, how well known he was and how people ate up every piece of gossip about him, they would have had a field day with this information, and Bear's life would have turned into a living hell.*

Little wonder he guarded his privacy jealously.

Thankfully he could afford to protect Randy from all this, give him the care and love he needed, and it was his money that allowed him to do it.

. . .

It took them over an hour to reach the house, and when Alina got her first glimpse of it she smiled. It wasn't anything like what she'd expected.

A beautiful modern work of art, it was built high upon a cliff overlooking the ocean.

Created from huge pieces of golden brown rock and beautiful light-colored wooden beams, the side of the house facing the water seemed to be one continuous huge sheet of glass.

It wasn't of course.

As they drove closer she could see that shining metal rafters separated the floors, and next to the main house stood a miniature version of it.

Also, very beautiful, it was set in its own garden with a high stone wall giving it privacy.

"This is beautiful Bear." She sighed, looking at him happily, "Just beautiful."

"Yes, it is." He agreed, smiling at her. "A friend of mine, a very talented architect, designed this for me. I think it's definitely his best work."

"Once it was completed and decorated, before my brother moved in, I allowed him to have it photograph, and to show it as part of his portfolio with the understanding that he would never reveal where it was built, and he never has."

"This design has drawn a lot of praise for him, even

gotten him a design award or two. It's been in Architectural digest as well, but he's never revealed its whereabouts."

"Rex is a good friend." He added quietly. "We went to Harvard together. I see him every now and then when I'm in New York."

As they walked up to the front door, a smiling middle-aged woman opened it.

"Mr. Bear, how are you?" she asked him, smiling

"Great Jenna, and you and Andy?"

"Wonderful as always." She replied, still smiling.

Bear introduced Alina, and as Jenna led them into the house she saw that it was just as beautiful inside as it was out.

Decorated with sleek modern furniture to match the style of the house, the living room Jenna led them into was filled with sunlight, and the floor to ceiling windows showed of the stunning ocean view.

As they walked into the room, Alina saw a man sitting in a wheelchair, his face frowning with concentration, working with a lump of clay on a tray attached to his chair.

"Hi there bro," Bear greeted him warmly, and he bent down to give him a hug while Randy smiled up at him happily.

The love between the two men was so evident Alina could feel her eyes tearing.

This man might not have had much love growing up, but Bear was certainly making up for it now.

"What's that you're making?" Bear asked him, his hand on his shoulder.

"A vase." Randy answered happily. "Jenna's showing me how."

"And he's doing a good job too." Jenna said coming up to him and smiling at him, then bending down so she could look at him at his own level she asked him,

"Ready for your snack?"

"Oh yeah." He grinned happily. "Can I have peanut butter and jelly again?"

"Strawberry jam or grape jelly?" she asked him, still smiling.

"Grape." He grinned. "I love grape."

"I know you do." Jenna replied, grinning at him. "I'll be right back." Then with a parting smile at them, she walked out to what Alina assumed must be the kitchen.

Bear looked at Alina and smiled.

"This is Ally. Randy." He said. "She's a friend of mine."

"High Ally." He said, looking at her happily. "Do you like vases?"

"Yup, I sure do." Alina said smiling back at him. Can I look at yours?"

"Sure." He agreed, then he frowned. "But it's not very good. Jenna says I have to practice."

"I think it's wonderful." Alina replied, looking at it, then looking back at him. "I love pink. It's one of my favorite colors."

"Me too." He replied happily.

They talked for a few more minutes then Jenna came in with his snack. He attacked it greedily, and when he was finished, he licked his fingers.

"I love peanut butter and jelly." He said happily.

"Me too." Alina agreed, smiling back at him. "Me too,"

They visited for about half an hour then Jenna came in and told them it was time for Randy's nap. After Bear hugged him again, kissing him softly on the forehead, she rolled him out of the room while they watched.

As he was still standing there, watching them make their way down the hall, Alina came up and kissed him on the cheek.

"You're right Bear," she whispered softly. "He's special. Very special."

"Yes, he is." Bear agreed, then turning to her with a smile he kissed her softly on the lips. Looking deeply in her eyes, he stroked her face.

"Thank you Ally." He said quietly. "You have no idea how much it means to me that you wanted to come with me today.

"Don't thank me Bear," she replied, looking at him lovingly, "It was a privilege and one I won't soon forget."

His eyes glistening with tears now, he softly bent his head and kissed her again.

. . .

On the drive back, he was quiet for the first half of the journey, obviously thinking, and Alina didn't mind. She wanted to think as well.

The more she learned about Bear the more she loved him.

She still couldn't believe what a man of extremes he was. One day he could be so loving and the next so cold and ruthless, but she was slowly starting to think that the loving side by far outweighed the other.

By the time they had been traveling for half an hour Bear's mood had changed and they laughed and joked as he maneuvered the battered jeep on the mud-covered roads.

There had obviously been rain during the night, something that was very common, and there were still puddles of water in the ruts, splashing up on the side of the car as they drove along.

THIRTY-SIX

They had left early in the morning and Bear had an appointment in the village at noon, so he dropped Alina at the school where she'd offered to help Jimena inventory supplies.

The students were all outside, enjoying the hot weather, and she smiled at a few of them as they waved at her, and waved back.

As she walked into the cool building she saw that Emanuel was sitting on one of the desks and he grinned as she walked in.

"Just waiting for teach." He said, still grinning, "She's outside with the kids for another half hour."

As Alina smiled and settled herself down at the desk to fill out some forms, he spoke, his voice serious now.

"Can I talk to you Alina?" he asked quietly.

"Sure." She replied, surprised.

He stopped then, obviously uncomfortable, and sighed, then looking at her resolutely he continued.

"I don't know if you know this, but Bear and I, well we've known each other for a long, long time. Since he was here with the Peace Corp in fact. We've always been good friends, and we talk about things." He smiled then, sheepishly.

"There aren't many people a man can feel comfortable talking to, but just as with women, sometimes it helps."

He had her full attention now, and as she sat up and looked at him, he smiled and softly spoke.

"You know he and I are pretty much involved together in just about everything that happens here. That whole thing with Diego. I had him checked out and once Bear decided what he wanted to do I ordered the boat."

He leaned towards her then, serious now.

"He told me you overheard their conversation and told me how you reacted."

He sighed.

"Bear's not as cold and ruthless as he seems."

"When he first came here he worked with a contractor who lied to him and swindled him out of a huge amount of money. It taught him a valuable lesson, and Bear is a man who takes lessons to heart. He never forgot that, and since then he's been adamant about honesty. He won't put up with anything underhanded, and personally, I think it's one of his best qualities."

He was still looking at her, and as he stopped, he searched her eyes.

"I don't know what you thought he did, but he was a lot more lenient than that man deserved. Personally, I would have probably strung him up in a tree if he'd done to me what he was trying to do to Bear. Just because the man has money is no reason to think you have a right to steal it."

"Bear's always fair. I've never seen him use anyone or mistreat them. He always pays fair wages. But he won't put up with dishonesty and he doesn't want dishonest people living on his island."

"He had the boat take him and his family to a neighboring island. He lined up a job for him there and a home. And before he left he had me give that man his last paycheck, so he would have something to start him off. That was a hell of a lot more than I would have done for that little weasel, you can be sure of that."

Emanuel was looking at her now, obviously deciding about something, then having made up his mind he continued, determined now.

"This is none of my business, I know. But he's a good man Alina,"

Looking her in the eyes, he added.

"and he loves you. I've never Known him to feel that

way about any other woman before. Please give him a break."

Walking towards the door, he put his hand on her shoulder when he passed her.

"I'm sorry if I spoke out of line, but he's my friend, and it needed to be said."

Then he turned with determination towards the door and went out to look for his wife.

* * * *

Alina sat there for a long time, just staring ahead.

Her mind was a total jumble.

It seemed this man was never what he seemed.

She'd thought him to be an irresponsible playboy, an uncaring ruthless business man, and in both cases, she'd been wrong.

She was slowly finding out just how wrong, and her mind was a confusing whirlwind of thoughts as she tried desperately to think about what she'd learned about him that day, what the real truth was about this man, and how it affected the way she really felt about him.

She'd never been able to understand how he could be so ruthless, so driven.

How he could be so cold and seemingly uncaring, but she was beginning to see now that just as her initial judgment of his character had been totally wrong, so too she'd been wrong about this.

He wasn't really cold or unfeeling. In fact, he was the total opposite. What Emanuel had told her had really opened her eyes.

Yes, he was still very demanding, still wouldn't put up with dishonesty of any kind, but she now knew why.

He'd seen how it could destroy, and he was doing what he could to protect himself and the ones he loved.

Could she really fault him for that?

Unlike how it had looked, and even though he'd definitely ended up losing his temper and scared her, his actions had been methodical, well-thought out, and yes, compassionate.

Even though this man had obviously been stealing from him, even though many men would have lashed out in anger, the only think he'd done was remove him from his life, so he would never have to deal with him again.

He'd sent him away, but he'd also provided him with a job, a home, and money with which to start again.

Where those the actions of a ruthless, uncaring man?

When she'd first come here she'd really known nothing about his life. It had been something completely foreign to her, something that she totally didn't understand, but she was slowly beginning to understand.

She'd been wrong about this man in so many ways.

Yes, he still had a lot of qualities she didn't like, but who was perfect?

What she needed to do was concentrate on his good points, and the way he loved and cared for his brother was definitely one of his very best qualities.

THIRTY-SEVEN

She knew now that Bear was passionate about sailing, that it gave him the break he so obviously needed from all his cares and responsibilities but try as she might she couldn't make herself feel anywhere as passionate about it as he did.

Bear was an expert sailor, she didn't doubt it, and going out with him was pleasant and she enjoyed it.

But she couldn't forget that storm.

Each time they went out she made herself trust him, didn't let herself get anxious about it. But she was never really successful.

She made herself go out with him a few times a week. She wanted to spend time with him and the boat was where he spent a lot of his off time, so that is what she had to do as well.

She was sure that given enough time she would probably relax, but right now she definitely didn't find it at all relaxing, regardless of how enjoyable the time they spent together ended up being.

She didn't really enjoy it, would never really enjoy it, but because she loved him she tried.

She told herself to concentrate on how happy it obviously made him. This is how he loved to relax, it gave him immense pleasure and she wanted to see him happy, but each time she went out she knew yet again that she could very easily live without this experience.

More than easily.

Even worse than being on the water with him was waiting for him.

She'd made the mistake of doing some research online, wanting to reassure herself that what Bear had told her was true, the sailboat was safe, and she didn't need to worry, but it seemed that in reality this was far from true.

Yes, his boat was one of the best, equipped with the latest equipment and everything it could have to make it as totally safe as possible, allow it to weather any storm, but this wasn't a guarantee he would always return.

Not by a long shot.

When she'd checked the manufacturer's website and read in more detail about this boat, it had definitely been reassuring.

It was an expensive model, made to order, and it was true. It was as safe as a boat could be, but when she checked the other websites about sailing she soon found out that "Safe" in the sailing world was a relative term.

Yes, when it came to being prepared you probably couldn't be more prepared in any other boat, but the bottom line was there were still accidents, still deaths, and it made her blood run cold reading about them.

As she read about all the men and women who had died on the water, people who were very well trained, often participating in races, she got more and more scared.

Every time she finished an article she told herself not to read any more, that this wasn't helping, but it was too late.

She knew now, and she couldn't forget that she knew.

And there were many days when he went out without her.

He would come home, obviously happy and renewed, anxious to make love to her, and she went to him willingly, just thankful that he'd returned, but day after day as she waited, as the fear built inside her, each time, along with loving him she started to hate him as well.

How much longer could she take this?

Living with this fear on a constant basis. Hating the experience, hating him more each time she had to go through it.

Could she keep doing this without eventually going crazy?

Eventually ending up hating him more than loving him?

. . .

But she kept all this fear to herself. She was determined that she wasn't going to ruin the one thing in his life that allowed him to relax and forget his cares.

She couldn't do that to him and she never would, but what about what this was doing to her?

She knew that many people enjoyed sailing and most of the time it really was safe. If you were careful and smart, you could usually avoid any danger, but she also knew that the ocean had a mind of its own, and it could change its mind in an instant.

As she herself had experienced, great weather could quickly turn to bad, and if he was far from shore as they had been he would be forced to ride it out again.

The thought absolutely terrified her, but she also knew that if she really wanted this relationship to go anywhere she would have to find some way to deal with it.

Others did, and she would have to as well, but was it worth it?

That was something she still couldn't answer.

The day after their visit to Randy, as she watched Bear getting out of bed, she could see he had something on his mind, and all through breakfast he still seemed to be thinking about it.

Finally, he sighed and looked at her.

"I'm not that busy this morning Ally and there's something I really have to think through. I'm going to go sail for a few hours. Do you need me to drop you off at the school?"

. . .

"No," she replied, trying to look happy and smiling, "I'll take the other jeep. I'm not sure how long I'll be."

"Okay", He grinned, "See you later then love."

And still grinning he walked out of the door, obviously looking forward to his day on the water.

And so, it starts again, she thought to herself, *The waiting and the fear*.

She made herself concentrate on her work that morning, finally finishing the last few small articles Gerald had asked for, then closing her laptop she walked out to the jeep.

She was working with the older students today and she really enjoyed this. Even though the young kids were a joy, seeing the older ones gradually improve their writing with her help and guidance was definitely very rewarding.

Just concentrate on that, she told herself. *If this relationship is going to have a chance in hell of working, then you've got to learn to cope just as hundreds of other women do.*

All afternoon she worked with them on the village website, and when the school day ended, she realized with surprise that she hadn't actually thought about him at all the last few hours.

Was she finally getting used to this?

Was it finally starting to get better?

She was pretty sure it was never going to go away, this fear, but maybe she could actually learn to cope.

· · ·

When he finally returned she could tell by his face that the day of sailing had done him good.

Whatever had been bothering him he had obviously had time to think through, and he was back to his usual cheerful self, laughing and joking with Melina as she brought him some tea.

"It was gorgeous on the water today," he said, sighing with obvious pleasure. "And it looks like it's going to be a gorgeous evening. I'm going to ask the band to play for us again."

Then he grinned wickedly at her.

"And wear that red dress. The one that makes you look so fuckable. We'll dance again, and I can think about taking it off you later."

He's definitely back to normal, she thought to herself, as she smiled at him. *That's obviously what he needed. I'm just going to have to cope.*

Dinner was amazing as always and as she danced in his arms while he pressed his body against hers, obviously ready for the second part of the evening, she sighed to herself with pleasure.

Yes, there were definitely things she wasn't crazy about when it came to this man, but there were also a lot that she loved, that she was starting to think it was going to be very hard to live without.

THIRTY-EIGHT

He made love even more passionately to her the next morning, and when he'd finally collapsed on his pillow, spent once again, he lay there with his eyes closed for a couple of minutes, then he turned to her, looking deep into her eyes.

"I love you so much Ally," he said softly, then stroking her hair, his face changed, and looking serious now he whispered.

"I think it's time."

He sat up then, and she sat up next to him, wondering what he was talking about.

Time?

Time for what?

He looked at her again, then turned and removed a black jewelry case from his bedside drawer.

"It's time Love." He said again, quietly, and his eyes were deadly serious now.

"I've been thinking about this ever since I took you up to see Randy." Then he sighed and looked away.

"Shit. I know I'm going to make a mess of this. It's not like I've had any experience."

He looked back at her seriously, searching her eyes.

"I know you've finished your assignments now. I know Gerald is expecting you back next week, but I don't want you to go.

You're too important now for me to let you go. And I can't see that ever changing.

Will you stay Ally?

Will you stay and marry me?"

She looked at him, totally surprised.

"Marry you?" she asked. "You want me to marry you?"

He was grinning now, obviously relieved he'd finally said it.

"Yes Love. That's what I said. Marry me."

Turning serious again, he added,

"I know I'm not a great bet. I know it won't be easy, for either of us. But I love you. I love you more than I thought it was ever possible to love anyone, and the thought of you leaving ... well I just can't bear it."

He grinned again.

"So, I really have no choice. This is the only way I can tie you down."

. . .

He looked searchingly into her eyes now.

"What do you say Ally? Are you willing to take a chance on me?"

He opened up the jewelry case he was still holding.

"This was my grandmother's engagement ring. As I've told you she was a wonderful lady. If you prefer I'll buy you something new. But it would give me great pleasure if you'll wear it. The two of you .... Well, other than my mother, who truthfully, I barely even remember, you are the only women I've ever loved. And ever plan to love." He added, kissing her then.

"I've been thinking about what you told me about your family.

That's what I want Ally," he said quietly, looking searchingly into her eyes.

"I want you to have my babies. Two or three off them. I want a home filled with love like what you grew up in.

Do you think we can create one together Ally?

More than anything, I know now that's what I really want."

Softly, he stroked her hair.

"I know this is a shock Love." He said, looking at her lovingly. "I don't want to put you on the spot. I know you. You need time to think about it."

He kissed her again.

"I'm not perfect Ally as you know too well." He said, sighing. "But I love you. Hopefully that's enough."

He handed her the box.

"Put this on your night table. You can let me know what you decide tonight."

Then giving her one last kiss, he got out of bed and headed for his dressing room.

THIRTY-NINE

Alina stood on the terrace, leaning on the stone wall.

The stone felt cool under her fingers as she looked out on the view.

Bear had left her early, giving her a quick kiss, then grabbing his jeans and a T-shirt he'd hurried out to join the rest of his crew.

Soon she'd have to dress as well.

She'd promised to help at the school again today and Jimena would be waiting for her, but first, while she finished her coffee, she needed to think.

Bear was working with his men on the far side of the island today, so she was alone. He wouldn't be back for hours, she knew.

There was still so much to do, and he was determined to do everything he could to help.

It wasn't enough for him to just provide the money they

needed. He wanted to be personally involved, work together with the men he considered part of his family, and this compassion and caring was just one of the many things she loved about him.

As she looked down into the garden she saw that Emanuel and his garden crew were busy there already and they had made great inroads.

It would take a while for it to get back to where it had been before the storm, but now that all the debris had been removed it looked so much better.

They were rebuilding all the flower beds, planting new plants, and she knew that by next year everything would have regrown again.

Everything grew so quickly here in this climate.

There was no sign of the storm now, and in a month or so it would just be a memory. Something nobody thought about any longer.

Until the next one.

That was life on the island and the natives were all used to it.

When he saw her on the patio, Emanuel grinned and waved up at her and she waved back at him, smiling, as she remembered their last conversation.

He was very loyal, a loving husband and father, and a very good friend. What he'd told her about Bear had certainly made her see him in a totally different light.

He's a wonderful man, she thought. *I'm glad I got to know him.*

As she continued to look out on the garden, Alina thought about Bear's proposal.

It had been so totally unexpected.

She would never in a million years think a man like him would be willing to tie himself down.

And the fact that he also wanted to have a family with her just blew her mind, but he was constantly doing that she thought, smiling to herself.

She was constantly finding out more new and wonderful things about him.

But marry him? That was a big step.

She loved him. There was no doubt about that.

She loved him so much it scared her, but he was nothing like the man she'd pictured in her mind that she would end up with.

His was a high-powered world of mergers and buyouts. The sums of money he controlled were impossible for her to really comprehend.

When he was working he could be cold, ruthless and vindictive. She'd heard it for herself now enough times.

The way he dealt with the people who crossed him, the way he could be so unforgiving, so brutal, willing to do whatever it took to protect his assets, it made her cold just thinking about it.

Could she live with that side of him?

Even though she knew now that most of the time he was only protecting himself, only protecting the people he loved, did it really justify acting the way he did?

She just didn't know.

And this sailing thing?

As she thought about the storm they'd had to ride, how incredibly terrified she'd been, she felt herself feeling cold again.

That had been the most horrifying, frightening experience she'd ever had to live through.

She'd never felt very comfortable on the water in the first place, and after that, even though she'd made herself go out with him again, made herself act as if she enjoyed it, she'd still been scared, and probably would always be scared, every time she went out with him.

But he loved it.

It was a major passion with him. Out of all the things he did he loved this the most, but each time he went out, each time she waited for him to come back, she would remember that storm and it would make her scared.

Could she live with that?

Live with the constant worry?

. . .

He'd told her he wanted her to have his babies, wanted to have children with her. What she'd told him about her family and how she'd grown up had obviously affected him a great deal, and he wanted to experience that for himself.

No doubt he would try, would really do his best, but when it came down to it he'd never experienced that kind of life, had no idea of what demands would be made of him.

Was he really up to it?

Would he be up to providing the kind of loving home for his children that she'd had and wanted for them as well, or in the end would it always be up to her?

She knew he loved her, really believed that, but he was constantly surrounded by temptation.

There were many, many women, a lot of them much more beautiful and alluring than she was, and he had always had his choice.

Whenever he wanted a new woman all he had to do was snap his fingers and they would come more than willingly to his bed.

Each time he had to go away she knew he would be surrounded by them, knew that the desire for sex was always with him, and knew how incredibly hard it was for him to do without. All his life he'd been able to satisfy that desire whenever he felt it.

How long could he go without falling victim to it again?

Could their love really compete with that?

. . .

He was incredibly handsome and charming, incredibly wealthy, and had a huge sexual appetite. It wasn't likely that would diminish anytime soon.

Even though he was getting older, he wasn't the kind of man who would ever be willing to go without sex for long.

Would he eventually tire of her?

Want to go back to his playboy ways?

Who knew. It was possible. Anything was possible with this man.

He was opinionated, sure he was always right, always wanting his own way, often didn't take life very seriously, and more than anything he loved to make her angry.

There were days when he totally drove her up the wall.

Would he change?

Not bloody likely, she thought sadly, but then along with the traits she hated he also had many others she loved.

He was a man of such unbelievable extremes.

He could be cold, ruthless and vindictive, but he was also very honest, immensely compassionate, caring to the point of risking his life for those he cared about, incredibly intelligent, and, she had to face it, totally lovable.

If she stayed with him it wasn't going to be an easy life for her, that was for sure.

. . .

Life with him would be a total rollercoaster of ups and downs.

Sometimes, especially when he was out on the water again and she sat there waiting for him, scared to death, wondering if he would get back safely, she thought she really hated him for putting her through that.

At other times, seeing how much he cared for this island, how much of himself he willingly gave to the people he cared for, she loved him more passionately then she'd ever thought possible.

All her life she'd wanted what her parents had.

A nice, comfortable, stable life, a couple of kids, and a loving dependable husband who loved her as much as she loved him.

She'd never wanted lots of money or all the fancy trappings that money could provide. She'd wanted a comfortable secure life in which to raise a family.

She'd wanted a man she could count on.

With Bear, she never knew what the day would bring.

She never knew what to expect next, never knew where she was with him, and life with him was a constant adventure.

There would be no routine, no comfort, no security.

But there would always be love.

She couldn't count on anything from him .... other than his love. That she knew deep in her heart that she would always be able to count on, but was it enough?

. . .

She should probably walk away.

Look for someone more normal, someone more likely to end up giving her the kind of life she'd always wanted, but in the end, could she do it?

Could she make herself be sensible, take the smart, practical route, and give him up?

When it came down to it, could she turn her back on everything she'd known here?

Walk away and leave him?

Not bloody likely, she thought with a smile. *Not bloody likely.*

Having made up her mind, Alina walked up the stairs to the bedroom, and going over to her night table, opened the small jewelry case Bear had given her.

She knew now deep in her heart what she really wanted to do, knew it was the only option she'd ever really had, and smiling happily now, she put on the ring.

FORTY

It was after seven when Bear finally returned that night, cold, filthy, and starving.

It had been a long day.

He'd worked hard doing manual labor all day, stopping only to quickly eat the sandwiches Melinda had given him, and she could see he was tired, but he also seemed very content.

"How did it go today?" she asked him, smiling after she kissed him.

"Great." He said, "It's really coming along. We're going to have that section done in no time. "

Melinda came in then with a tray for him, and he ate greedily, then settled back with a sigh.

"I think I'm ready for an early night." He said, smiling,

then getting up he put his arm around her and walked her up the stairs.

When they entered the bedroom, he smiled at her again.

"Just going to have a quick shower. Why don't you take of your clothes while you wait," He said, grinning wickedly now. "It will save time."

She smiled to herself as she got into bed, pulling back the covers invitingly for him.

As he joined her he reached for her hungrily.

"It's incredible. I felt exhausted when I got home, but seeing you there, naked, waiting for me, suddenly I feel very energetic."

"Good," she whispered, smiling softly at him. "Take the pills. I think we've got some celebrating to do.

Then she showed him her hand, the diamond shining up at him as she held it to the light.

He looked at it for a long time, then he looked back at her, unsure.

"Does this mean what I think it means?"

"Yes," she answered, still smiling. "Yes, I'm going to marry you, so take those pills already. "

. . .

He grinned as he reached for the bottle and swallowed, then turning back to her, he gave her that famous sexy stare. The one she'd seen in so many magazines and looked at with such disgust before she'd met him.

The one she now loved.

"Looks to me like you never learned your lesson." He growled, "Didn't I tell you once before what would happen to you if you tried to boss me around again?"

She looked up at him and smiled.

"Yes, you did. But I forget. Maybe you'd better remind me."

Groaning, he moved over her, his eyes dark with desire, and taking full advantage of the pills, he made her come over and over again, losing all track of time, the feeling so intense that at times he didn't think he could stand it, as he felt her tighten around him, convulsing, her whole body vibrating, while she screamed and moaned with pleasure.

Finally dropping onto his pillow, totally exhausted, too worn out to even open his eyes, he fought to catch his breath.

"Fuck!" he exclaimed, when at last he was able to speak.

After a minute, he'd recovered enough to opened them, and he looked at her.

She was still catching her breath, and he softly stroked her face, grinning.

. . .

"Fuck." he said again, looking into her eyes.

"That was bloody fucking amazing. And to think I'll be able to do this now whenever the hell I want."

"Fuck!"

THE END

DO ME A FAVOR?

I hope you've enjoyed reading my book.
I loved writing it because Billionaires and Happy Endings
are so my thing!

If you'd like to help me get more readers,

please write me a review on Amazon.
Just a line or two will do.
I read them all,
and they really do make a big difference,
especially for us self-published authors!

HERE'S AN SNEAK PEEK FROM
ANOTHER BOOK IN THE SERIES ....

Seduced
by the
Billionaire
Billionaire Adventurers
Harriet Pope

Even though on the surface her life was fun and exciting, deep down Ellen lived in the past. Could she find her way out of it and into Love?

Ellen had lived an exciting life. She'd worked for an airline and travelled around the world meeting a lot of people and having affairs with a lot of men.

She told herself she was happy. She had an interesting life, an interesting career, and lots of friends, but deep in her heart she knew, as she'd always known, that it really wasn't enough.

When she'd been very young she'd met her mentor. He'd been an amazing man. Rich, smart, and incredibly sexy and they'd had an amazing eight-month love affair together. But then he'd had to leave.

He was married, had children and commitments, and she didn't fit into his life long-term.

She'd known that from the beginning, but she hadn't realized how much it would hurt. How much everything he'd taught her would influence her life from then on.

Now she was a decade older and presumably wiser but was she really? She'd never been able to commit to a relationship since, and though she'd enjoyed her life, she was still basically alone.

That much older now, she no longer wanted to be. Short term lovers just didn't do it for her any longer. She wanted, needed, more.

Could she find someone to love again, or was she forever going to dwell on what she wished could have been.

To read an excerpt, turn the page ....

CHAPTER 1

Ellen lay back in the tub.

The water was hot, the sweet scent of roses and lavender surrounded her, and the glass of wine on the little table within her reach was cold and delicious.

Was there a better way to end the day?

It had been a day of revelations. Of secrets revealed and emotions once firmly checked now allowed to spill out into the light of day.

It had been a good day.

Much better than she'd ever believed possible.

As she lay back in the tub, music playing softly in the background she knew she'd been incredibly blessed.

She took a sip of the cold wine, closed her eyes, and cast her mind back. Back to when it had all begun.

* * * *

She'd started working for the airline in 1972.

She'd been offered two different jobs, and if she'd taken the other one, the one she'd really wanted, her life would have gone in a different direction and been completely different.

She still remembered the day she'd made that decision.

Ellen had loved both of her parents, but she and her father had been particularly close.

He'd trained as an architect at the Sorbonne in Paris, and as a child she'd loved to look at the old notes and drawings he still had stashed away in a box in the basement.

He was creative, very artistic, and she'd inherited that same creative gene from him, so it was only natural that she would want to follow in his footsteps.

Even though she would have loved to study Architecture just as he had, in those days there were very few women architects and seeing it would be a hard road for her to follow her father had discouraged her, encouraging her to study drafting instead.

Along with being creative she was also very logical, so this was a great field for her and she enjoyed it, was exceptionally good at it, and was looking forward to finally getting out and working.

Her course offered a placement service and as part of the process she was required to take some tests.

When she'd gone in to get her results, she'd received the news that would change the direction of her life.

. . .

She'd been offered a very good position at a local architecture firm as a draftsperson, but she'd also been offered a position with a major airline in a completely unrelated line of work.

It seemed that her scores in the particular area of interest to them had been exceptional, and they wanted to recruit her as one of their trainees in the brand-new computer department they were setting up in Montreal.

Since her family lived in Winnipeg and she'd lived there most of her life as well, this would be a major move.

As with all important decisions in her life so far, Ellen discussed it with her father.

He'd always been her guiding light and had never steered her wrong and she trusted his advice.

He'd been surprised, just as she'd been at the offer, but just as she was he was a very logical as well as very intelligent man. After talking to some of his engineer friends who knew more about that whole field, he'd told her she should grab the opportunity and go with it.

At the time, for a young person working for an airline was a very prestigious job.

It had a lot of benefits, but the best known of these were all the free passes she would be entitled to receive for both herself and her family.

Other than one of the few office jobs available to women, the best chance a woman had of working for them was as a flight attendant.

. . .

One of her friends had applied and she'd listened with amusement to the tails she'd told her.

Having to work at a job where you had your weight and measurements taken every month and were expected to stick within strict guidelines hadn't sounded like much fun to her. Neither had serving meals and drinks and cleaning up messes, but each to their own she'd decided. I

t certainly wasn't something she would ever be inter-ested in doing, but this was different.

From what Ellen had been told, she was only one of two women who'd been offered this opportunity.

One of her father's engineering friends who kept up with modern developments had told him that computers would be the future and she would be crazy not to take advantage of the job offered to her, so she had, and it had turned out to be a very smart move.

The computer industry expanded over the next few years by leaps and bounds and her career expanded with it.

Meanwhile the drafting job that she'd loved gradually disappeared, swallowed up by the new technology that she'd now become part of creating.

* * * *

One of the first things she did with her passes was to take both of her parents on a vacation.

Her father had wanted to visit France again, and they'd spent a few great weeks there together, visiting some of his old haunts.

He'd introduced her to some of his friends in Paris, and after a week of sight-seeing they'd spent a week in Nice with one of his old friends who he hadn't seen since the war.

Travel wasn't something normal everyday people did on a regular basis yet, and it had made her very happy to know she could provide her father with this pleasure.

Since Winnipeg had to be one of the coldest places in the country in Winter, her mother had loved the idea of going somewhere warm, so she'd arranged a trip to Mexico for them.

They'd spent several days exploring the jungle pyramids on the Yucatan peninsula before flying to Acapulco and then ending up in Mexica City.

It was when they were shopping on their last day that the first incident that she could remember happened.

She was looking at something in a store window, and as she turned back to look at her mother who'd stopped to look at something half a block away, she noticed that she was speaking to a very handsome man and she was smiling.

Since they didn't know anyone in the city, she looked at him with interest. He was tall, well-built and very good looking, probably in his early forties, with dark hair and impeccably dressed in a suit and carrying a briefcase of some kind, so obviously a businessman.

He looked up at Ellen with dark brooding eyes, then after a minute he smiled and bowed his head. Then he tipped his hat to her mother and walked off.

. . .

Her mother was laughing when she walked up to her.

"Well, that was pretty unbelievable." She said, smiling at her.

"Maybe this kind of thing happens in Mexico all the time, but I have to say I've never heard of anything like this."

Ellen looked at her curiously.

"Who was he? What did he say to you?"

Her mother turned, still smiling, and indicated his now receding figure as he walked away from them and then greeted another man before both of them entered one of the large office buildings.

"You see that guy there? He stopped me in the middle of the street to tell me I had a very beautiful daughter."

"What?" Ellen said in surprise. "He really said that?"

"Yes." Her mother laughed. She was obviously getting a real kick out of it. Then her manner changed.

"You're very attractive, of course, but nobody would call you beautiful." She studied her thoughtfully.

"Obviously you have something though Ellen. I've never heard of a man stopping in the middle of the street like that before."

She laughed again.

"Good thing you have a chaperone, isn't it?" she said, taking her by the arm.

Ellen had to smile. She was kidding, right?

After spending a couple of years at University and working for a year she was no innocent.

She'd had several boyfriends, and even lived with one for a few months, so she was just as experienced as any normal twenty-three-year-old girl was in those days, but she and her mother had never had the kind of relationship where they could talk about things like that.

They spent the rest of the afternoon shopping, sight-seeing and enjoying themselves, but later, while they were having coffee and cakes in one of the many sidewalk cafes, she noticed her Mom looking at her quizzically, and it made her slightly uncomfortable.

It had definitely been a strange incident, but they never mentioned it again, and as they continued to enjoy their vacation together, she soon put it out of her mind.

She hadn't thought of that for years, Ellen thought, but now that she was trying to decide just how much of what the Mor Doo had said had actually come true, she remembered it, and thinking about it, that had probably been the first time she could remember that this whole thing about men had really started to show itself.

CHAPTER 2

Ellen spent six months training, then she started to work.

It was all new, different, and very exciting.

Living in Montreal was a great experience. It was a very cosmopolitan city and even though she spoke only the minimal French she'd learned in school, it wasn't really necessary to be able to speak any more.

This was before the changes in the laws, and the majority of the city was still English speaking and filled with many large companies from all over the world, each of which brought its own international flavor.

She found that she loved her work, and in many ways, it suited both her logical and creative side.

She worked with twelve men and one woman, Neely, who was originally from Thailand, and they all worked hard and played hard.

. . .

That was just how life was.

They were all single, she made a lot of good friends, and mostly she was treated fairly, but there was still a lot of prejudice against women, and she had to work twice as hard as her co-workers and even that didn't always guarantee that she would get the acknowledgement she deserved.

One of the few married people in her department was her project manager, a middle-aged Frenchman.

Originally from Tangiers, He and his family had lived in Montreal for many years, and he'd been instrumental in the startup of their department.

He was dark and quite good looking in that Mediterranean sort of way with curly black hair, dark eyes, and a cheerful personality.

A decade older than she was, he lived with his wife and young children in a high-rise apartment in the city center.

They'd gotten along together well from the start and he'd taken her under his wing, giving her interesting assignments and guiding her when there was some new application she had to learn.

After a year she'd been recommended for a promotion along with another man in her department, and he'd told her she was bound to get it since she was so much better at what she did than he was, but it hadn't happened.

The day he'd called her into his office to let her know, he'd been angry, and she could see just how annoyed and frustrated he was.

. . .

"I fought for you Ellen." He'd said with a sigh, "but some of those bastards, well, they have a lot of preconceived ideas. Mon Dieux (My God) Doug is going to be a disaster in that position, but would they listen to me? Non (no)."

She was sitting across from him at his desk, her hands lying on a folder she'd brought with her, and he had leaned over and placed his hands on top of hers.

"You know Ellen, if I had your looks I'd give up this whole fucking business and go out and work the streets. At least there you know a woman like you would be more than appreciated."

Then he sat back in his chair.

"I'm really sorry." He said with a sigh. "You are definitely the best person for that job."

"It's okay, Rene." She'd said to him. "I know you did your best for me, and I appreciate it."

Giving him a smile to show her appreciation for his efforts, she got up and walked out of his office.

Thinking about it now, Ellen had to laugh at how inappropriate that whole conversation had been.

She knew that he would never have made a remark like that today or put his hands on her, but that had been a whole different time. She'd understood that he was trying to make her feel better in his own way, and she'd appreciated that he cared.

. . .

It had all worked out in the end.

After a few more months, a position had become available in Toronto, and Rene had made sure she'd gotten it.

She'd been transferred there, the company had paid for the move and helped her find an apartment, and she had started on yet another stage of her life.

She was sorry to leave Montreal and the friends that she'd made, but Toronto was another new and exciting world, she was young, and her life with all its new experiences stretched out in front of her.

* * * *

It was inevitable that she and Neely would become good friends working together the way they did, and that friendship lasted even after she was transfer to her new position.

Neely was not only very bright but also had a great personality, and they often laughed together about some of the things the men they worked with would say or do.

Both of them tended to work for weeks on a project, working around the clock for six days a week, then they would be given a week or two off before the new project began.

That's when she would take one of the stack of tickets she had stashed in her desk drawer at home and fly somewhere for a break.

It was one of these times that Neely invited her to fly home with her to Thailand.

She had family who still lived there, and since it sounded like it could be a great trip, Ellen agreed and looked forward to it eagerly.

Neely's family was warm and welcoming and made Ellen feel right at home, and she enjoyed the whole trip very much. A few days before they were to leave, Neely told her she was going to go see a Mor Doo and asked her if she wanted to go with her.

At first Ellen thought she was talking about just some local fortune teller and thought she was doing it for a lark, but Neely soon put her straight.

"This isn't just a fortune teller Ellen." She told her. "A Mor Doo is much more than that. They are doctors. Doctors who can see the future, and many people here go to visit them on a regular basis and take them very seriously.

There's just one thing about this one we're going to see. You have to make sure you wear only white."

"Why?" Ellen asked curiously.

"I don't know." Neely replied. "That's just the way it is. Everyone there wears white, they insist upon it, and he won't see you if you don't."

It all sounded a bit strange, but Ellen had always been game to try new things and she willingly went along with it.

* * * *

One thing Ellen found very interesting were all the beautiful temples in Bangkok. They had toured several, and she'd been amazed at how intricately constructed they were, and the one Neely took her to was no exception.

She'd made an appointment for them, and they were shown into a large room where an old monk with gray hair that had turned almost completely white and wearing a white robe, sat on a large golden richly carved and very ornate chair.

Next to him stood two attendants, also in white robes, and a couple of white tigers with black and brown stripes lay quietly at his feet.

Ellen looked at them with alarm.

"Tigers?" she whispered to Neely. "Really?"

Neely laughed.

"Don't worry. They're very tame."

"Yeah, right." Ellen muttered to herself, but she'd come so far, and those guys didn't seem worried, so, still a bit anxious, she nevertheless followed Neely to where she stopped just in front of the monk.

He watched them as they walked in, then, once they reached his chair, he quietly indicated the stools that had been placed in front of him and gestured to them to sit.

Ellen kept eyeing the tigers, not really trusting them, but neither one of them had moved.

They just sat there looking at her with beautiful big eyes and gradually she relaxed.

How bad could it be? Those guys were still alive and didn't seem worried.

After talking to Neely for a few minutes, he turned to Ellen and looked at her with interest. She hadn't understood anything that had been said, so she looked at Neely questioningly.

"How will I know what he's saying?" she asked.

"Don't worry." Neely answered quietly. "I'll translate."

The monk took her hand and held it while he stared at her thoughtfully, and after a couple of minutes she started to feel a bit uncomfortable, but he kept softly holding her hand and looking at her with a strange look on his face.

Finally, he spoke, and as he did, Neely translated.

"You will be fine." He said quietly. "You will always be surrounded by men and money. You will be fine."

He stopped then, but he kept looking at her and then he spoke again.

"Men will be your teachers little one. They will teach you, desire you, love you, and sometimes hurt you very badly, but in the end a man will be your salvation. Soon you will marry and have children, but your life will be different from most.

You will be much older before you reach the best part of it.

In this life, men will be everything to you and you will

be everything to them. They are how you will learn every-thing you're here to learn."

Then after giving her one last look, he got up, and with the assistance of his helpers, he walked out of the room, his tigers following him, and leaving them sitting there staring after him.

They just sat there for a minute, then Neely turned to her.

"Wow." She said. "That sounded deep. I wonder what he meant?"

"Yes, I wonder." Ellen thought.

Looking back, Ellen still wasn't sure what it was he'd been saying to her.

She'd questioned her again, but Neely had insisted that was the exact translation of what he'd said.

Her life would be different than most, and she would be much older before she reached the best part of it. Men would be her teachers, they would be everything to her and she would be everything to them, and she would be surrounded by them all her life.

It had been a very strange prediction, but as she looked back Ellen could see that in many ways it had certainly been true.

WANT MORE HARRIET POPE BOOKS?

Visit my website
harrietpope.com
for Sneak Peeks of all my books.

Meanwhile,
Turn the page for a full list
and a couple of **FREE** novels ....

EVERGREEN COVE SERIES

If you like Small Town Romance
with hot sexy heroes
you'll love the Evergreen Cove Series!

Small Town Artist - the first book introduces the Series
& explains why Jessy started to do her house drawings.

Even though there is an order to this Series, all the books can be read as standalone.

Book 1 - Small Town Artist
Jessy & Kevin's story
(A Friends to Lovers Next Door Neighbor Romance).

Book 2 - Small Town Author
Janet & Allan's story
(A Second Chance Later in Life Silver Fox Romance)

Book 3 - Small Town Passions
Mac & Ellen's story
(A Second Chance Later in Life Silver Fox Romance)

Book 4 - Small Town Daddy
Brad & Melanie's story
(An Enemies to Lovers Second Chance Romance)

Book 5 - Small Town Lovers
Alexia & David's story
(A Second Chance Later in Life Silver Fox Romance)

Book 6 - Small Town Inspiration
Steve & Barb's story
(A Friends to Lovers Inspirational Keto Romance)

Book 7 - Small Town Forever Love
Susan & Bob's story
(A Second Chance Later in Life Silver Fox Romance)

Book 8 - Small Town Doctor
Amanda & Seth's story
(An Enemies to Lovers Keto Doctor Boss Romance)

All books are available in ebook and print.

DESERT SANDS TRILOGY

Love to read about
Hot Desert Sands and even hotter
Sexy Desert Sheiks?

try my
Desert Sands Trilogy

Book 1 - His Reluctant Guest
Sally & Hassim's story
(A Sheik Baby Romance)

Book 2 - His Defiant Lover
Belinda & Na'il's story
(A Sheik Enemies to Lovers Romance)

Book 3 - His Promised Bride
Sabrina & Alim's story
(A Sheik Second Chance Later in Life Silver Fox Romance)

To get the full story these books should be read in order

BILLIONAIRE ADVENTURERS

If you enjoy reading about Hot Sexy Powerful Billionaires
who live, love, and travel all over the world,
you'll love the Billionaire Adventurers Series.

These are all stand alone novels
and can be read in any order.

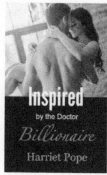 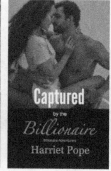 

Inspired by the Doctor Billionaire
Alex & Olivia's story
(A Second Chance Later in Life Keto Doctor Silver Fox
Romance)

Captured by the Billionaire
Carlos & Olivia's story
(An Enemies to Lovers Bandit Romance)

Played by the Billionaire
Elina & Bernard's story
(An Enemies to Lovers Island Romance)

 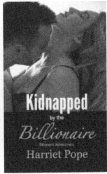 

Blackmailed by the Billionaire
Jana & Phill's story
(A Second Chance Enemies to Lovers Later in life Silver
Fox Romance)

Kidnapped by the Billionaire
Reb & Jake's story
(An Enemies to Lovers Biker Romance)

Seduced by the Billionaire
Francois & Ellen's story
(A Second Chance Later in Life Silver Fox Romance)

Like a couple of **FREE** Romance Books?

Small Town Artist is Jessy & Kevin's story
and the introduction to the Evergreen Cove series.
Here is the link.

Inspired by the Doctor Billionaire is the story of
Alex and Olivia and how they ended up in Mexico.
This is the first book in the Billionaire Adventurers series.
Here is the link

(If you are reading a print version of my book, just go to my
website www.harrietpope.com to get the links.)

Sign up for my mailing list
and I'll send you these books absolutely **FREE**!

Don't worry.

I'll only email you when I have something good to offer you like a new book, a **FREE** extra, or a **FREE** promotion, and of course you can unsubscribe at any time.

Are you into KETO?
A fan of Diet & Health Books?

I write non-fiction under my real name Joanna Alderson
at
www.joannaalderson.com

You'll find Sneak Peeks, recipes and more.

Meanwhile turn the page for a complete list
of my books
plus a couple of **FREE** ones
to get you started.

Keto Series
(8 Books)

Simple Keto for Beginners
Simple Keto after 50
Mediterranean Keto
Keto for Busy People

Keto Miracle Noodles
Keto Egg Fast
Keto Happy Hour Cookbook
Keto Holiday Recipes

Keto Fasting Series
(4 Books)

Fasting for Health & Weight Loss
Fasting & The Keto Diet
Keto Fasting A How To Manual

Keto Fasting 3 Books in 1 !

LCHF Series
(3 Book)

LCHF A Simple Guide
LCHF Quick & Easy Freezer Plan

LCHF 2 Books in 1 !

Diet & Exercise Tips Series
(2 Books)

How to Lose Weight.... FAST!
How to Lose Belly Fat.... FAST!

The perfect planners for your diet.
Contains a diet summary specifically for your diet
for you to reference at any time.
At 5 1/2" x 8 1/2" it's the perfect size
for your purse or briefcase.
It's a one month planner, but there are 4 pages for each day
so you could easily use it for up to 4 months.

Like a couple of **FREE** books?

If you're just starting Keto, or
considering starting
but have no idea how,
SIMPLE KETO FOR BEGINNERS
has all the info. you'll need to get going.

And if you're looking to make some changes in your life
and need some inspiration,
or if you're going through some bad times
and need something to cheer you up,
SIMPLE PLEASURES is for you.
It's full of great tips and tricks
that you can easily incorporate into your life,
and it's a quick read.
Get it here.

(If you're reading a print version of this book just go to
www.joannaalderson.com to get the links)

Sign up for my mailing list and
I'll send you these books absolutely **FREE**!

And don't worry.
I'll only email you when I have something good to offer you
like a new book, a **FREE** extra, or a **FREE** promotion,
and of course you can unsubscribe at any time.

DIET JOURNALS & PLANNERS

If you've ever had trouble keeping track of your shapeup progress,
look for my Diet Journals that I created
to go specifically with my books.

They are specially tailored
to your particular diet,
and include all the basics from the book
so you can easily check them.

For your convenience
they come in 2 sizes:
7" x 10"
(almost letter size for your briefcase)
and 5 " x 8 "
(the perfect half-page size for your purse or bag)

There's lots of room for listing what you eat, for adding
notes, a special section where you can keep track of your
exercise ....

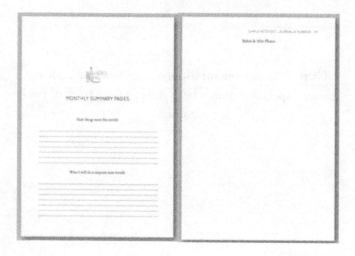

.... and there are even special pages
for notes on the recipes you've tried,
so you can easily reference these again.

At the end of each month you can summarize how you did
that month,
set goals for the next month,
and even put in some photos if you wish.

Each Journal gives you space
for 3 months of records
.... more than enough time
to create a healthy new eating habit!

You don't have to use a Journal to be successful,
but the Experts all agree that doing so
greatly improves
your chances for Success!

find me at :
www.HarrietPope.com
harrietpope@outlook.com

Made in the USA
Monee, IL
20 March 2025